An Ar _ _____untas Stories
by Vancouver Island Writers

"Plots in the Pantry" is a collaborative effort of Vancouver Island writers whose genres are wide-ranging, from science fiction to cookbooks. What they do have in common, however, is a love of writing, the beautiful part of the world they live in, and a love of Christmas.

What follows are eight Christmas stories, and eight Christmas recipes that refer *somehow* to food mentioned in the accompanying story. The stories take us from Nanaimo to El Salvador, the wilderness to the big city, 1926 to 2025, and feature characters from young to old, providing truly family reading.

"Plots in the Pantry" can be found both as an ebook and a paperback on Amazon (**www.amazon.com**), the "Writing in Progress" website (**www.wipqb.com**) as well as at each of the participating authors' websites. There is contact info for each author at the back of this book.

Thanks for reading and we hope you enjoy our work!

CONTENTS

Chapter One

KANAKA CREEK   *by Sandy Hunter*   4

Recipe for Santa's Favourite Hot Chocolate   13

Chapter Two

CHRISTMAS RUNAWAY   *by Mimi Barbour*   14

Recipe for Mimi's Homemade Bread   43

Chapter Three

FLASH   *by Clive Scarff*   44

Recipe for World Famous Nanaimo Bars   67

Chapter Four

CHRISTMAS MIRACLE   *by Hendrik Witmans*   68

Recipe for Impromptu Christmas Dinner   92

Chapter Five

A FATHER'S LOVE   *by Lorhainne Eckhart*   93

Recipe for Christmas Goose   104

Chapter Six

PIES FOR PERSONAL USE   *by Genevieve McKay*
106

Recipe for Blueberry Pie 117

Chapter Seven

TIT FOR TAT *by W.J.Merritt* 118

Recipe for Whipped Shortbread Cookies 129

Chapter Eight

SCREWGE: THE REDEMPTION OF RABBI
HAWKINS *by Jim Miller* 130

Recipe for Beer Steamed Lobster Tails   201

Author Contact Info   202

Kanaka Creek: copyright 2011 Sandy Hunter
Christmas Runaway: copyright 2011 Mimi Barbour
Flash: copyright 2011 Clive Scarff
The Christmas Miracle: copyright 2011 Hendrik Witmans
A Father's Love: copyright 2011 Lorhainne Eckhart
Pies for Personal Use: copyright 2011 Genevieve McKay
Tit for Tat: copyright 2011 W.J. Merritt
Screwge: The Redemption of Rabbi Hawkins: copyright 2011 Jim Miller

ISBN-13: 978-1466485778
ISBN-10: 1466485779

www.wipqb.com

Chapter One

KANAKA CREEK   *by Sandy Hunter*

The phone startled Jason into heart pounding awareness; realizing he was slapping at a silent alarm clock, he groped for the receiver.

Yvonne muttered into her pillow, "Whazzit...? Christmas Eve, don' they know."

Clearing his throat, Jason rasped, "Dr. Kay...". The green luminals of the tumbled bedside clock flashed 12:10 a.m.

"...Jason...it's Eva Clarkson...our Tinker has a Christmas ornament hook caught in his mouth. He's pawing at his poor face, but won't let us get near him ..."

"Uh-huh. S' O.K., Eva. Get Tinker to the clinic — don't try to remove the hook yourselves."

Yvonne's eyes squinted in the light of the bed table lamp. "Think you'll be long?"

Jason paused and untangled from shoving his two feet down a single pant leg. "Nope. Keep the bed warm."

"Mumph," she affirmed and curled into the vacated warm sport.

Jason yawned and massaged his scalp vigorously for two luxurious minutes.

By 1:15a.m. Eva Clarkson had been phoned and reassured as to Tinker's continuing prospects of a long and adventurous life. Jason checked one final time on his patient—Tinkerbell was sonorously sleeping-off the anaesthetic. As Jason locked the front door of the clinic behind him, he lifted his hand and traced the letters engraved on the new brass plate, Jason M. Kay, D.V.M., with a small jerk of his shoulder, he turned away.

Urging his old truck along the Lougheed Highway, he peripherally noted the beauty of this Christmas Eve night; the rural countryside of Maple Ridge lay frost-glinting under a pristine sky. The stars pulsed brightly as if fanned by the brisk wind blowing down the Fraser River.

On an impulse, he decided to take the old Kanaka Creek Road home, and turned north from the star-molten Fraser, into the silent woodlands lining the road's steeply sinuous ascent. He drove it with the casual ease of familiarity. His thoughts twisting through memories of Christmas past...

Dad's ropy arms lifting Laddie off the road with the same gentle care he used to carry baby Bridget to bed. The carload of revellers continuing to careen on down the country road. "There's nothing we can do, son, but put poor Lad out of his misery."

"No, Dad, no! That's all I'll ever want for Christmas, nothing else. Make Laddie be alright again!"

The Ford grumbled around a blind curve and the headlights caught a hay wagon and team halted immediately ahead, an old man was crouched alongside one of the horses.

Damn! Jason hit the brakes and cranked the wheel. A hay wagon! ...what the...! As the truck spun on the icy road, he registered a kaleidoscope of images: jittering horses, the old man's startled blue eyes, and tall cedar trees sparkling with fiery crystals. The drainage ditch gaped like black doom ahead. He dimly heard a shout as the front end of the truck tipped into blackness and his head struck the steering wheel.

***

"...my boy! Are you all right? Speak to me, lad!" A bluff, overloud voice dinned in his ears, Jason cracked one eye open. There, leaning in the door, was a beaming apparition straight from the pages of Norse folklore.

"...must be a concussion," Jason mumbled, fingering his forehead. "Ow...!"

The apparition's lively blue eyes sobered a moment and surveyed him. The vibrant skin crinkled into a smile again. "No, dear boy," the apparition stated, "you're just fine." The silver hair and beard nodded vigorously and the moonlight that aureoled his head was flung into the dark corners of the night.

An arm reached in and pulled Jason out of the car.

"Ow...no...Wait..." Jason swayed on his feet and eyed his rescuer dubiously. He saw he'd been wrong in estimating advanced age; this was a hale and hearty man in spite of the deceptive white hair. The burly fellow wore a whiter-than-white sweatshirt, and gaudy red pants held up by brilliant scarlet suspenders. Jason blinked painfully, tempted to leave his eyes shut. Everything about this hallucination was too bright, too loud, too...

Jason felt himself sway. Ol' Hearty grabbed his arm, "...here, young fellow," the old fellow grunted with effort, pushing Jason from behind, up and over the lip of the ditch, "over to the sled with you. I'll pour something that'll cheer you up."

Sled? The apparition forcefully propelled him over to what Jason incredulously recognized as a large red sled with eight gigantic reindeer milling about in loosened harness.

Jason gaped, weakly resisting as Ol'Hearty firmly propelled him forward. They crunched their way over the frosty pine needles. "Come, lad," the old fellow encouraged cheerfully.

Eight antlered heads swung toward Jason with a sound like wind through dry thickets. He sensed, rather than heard, voices.

"This is a very real hallucination I'm having..." Jason remarked to Ol'Hearty. He stared down into the old man's cheery face. Strange—he'd never realized that eyes really could twinkle. "...and just look who I'm talking to," Jason muttered to himself. Strange subliminal laughter accompanied Ol' Hearty's chuckle.

A thermos cup full of—Jason inhaled deeply—hot chocolate, was placed in his chilled hand. Mmmm—wonderful! Olfactory hallucinations also, Jason observed. "This is good..." I smell...cinnamon. And Chili ?

"Hallucinations, nothing!" boomed Jason's hallucination. "And yes, a pinch of chili makes all the difference, you know.

"Come now. You know very well who I am. But let's be introduced in proper form." The apparition shifted his steaming thermos to the left hand and extended his right. "Kris Kringle, dear boy, or Santa—if you prefer."

Jason shook hands, somewhat mechanically. "Jason Kay," he murmured.

"Well of course you are," interrupted Kris, "I knew that already. Here let me introduce the lads..."

"Wait—just wait a minute," Jason blurted,"I'm not one to be passing the time of day with a figment of my imagination, and I know you're an hallucination because before the accident and my head injury," Kris rocked on his heels, gazing with limpid politeness as Jason pointed to the bruise on his forehead, "I saw the hay wagon and an old man kneeling by what I'm sure were horses. Explain that!"

Kris Kringle waved a broad hand in abrupt dismissal. "A mere spell of disguise, my boy, hastily drawn at that.

"Spell...?" choked Jason, ducking the waving hand.

"It really is most opportune you've happened along," said Kris, placing the thermos back in the sled.

"Opportune?" repeated Jason, glancing back at the truck where it protruded from the ditch like a spent arrow.

Kris continued mildly,"Of course I should remember there is no such thing as coincidence...hmm..." he mused, laying a finger beside his nose and turning a sapient eye on the fuming doc.

"You grew up to be a veterinarian didn't you, Jason?"

Nonplussed, Jason stammered, "Of course...you'd know…you're my hallucination." He turned, hunching his shoulder. A surge of resentment swelled through him from some dark, bitter place he hadn't even been aware was there. "I don't believe in you." Jason was astonished at himself; he felt just like a disappointed child. He scowled at Santa.

Santa regarded the man before him. He nodded abruptly and sat on the running board of the sled, gesturing for Jason to sit beside him. The reindeer, quiet as smoke, drew about the two men. One reindeer shed a bright corona of light, so it seemed as if they sat under a street lamp, rather than in the dark backwoods of Kanaka Creek.

Jason hesitated, and then sat, his hands clasped, his eyes on the ground before him. "You are not real," he repeated.

"Of course I am," affirmed Santa kindly, "thoughts are things, my boy. Thoughts are things." Kris glanced again at Jason's averted face and shadowed eyes. He sighed. "These," his gesture took in the heavily loaded sled, "are material things, Jason, outward symbols of a spiritual giving of self. At least, it should be." For a moment, Kris's pose duplicated Jason's. "But then," he continued, "sometimes it is deemed best for a particular child to be given a greater gift—an opportunity to grow in spirit—and material things may be withheld, or taken away. It is up to that soul to find the deeper, truer meaning of the spirit-gift." Kris placed a heavy hand on Jason's shoulder. "Your Laddie gave up his life so that a young boy could find his life-path. This, I know," he added, shaking that resistant shoulder slightly. "Think now, Jason, when did you decide to be a veterinarian?"

Jason blurted a wry, incredulous laugh. Pressing his fingers against his eyes, he slowly shook his head. When he finally looked up, Santa raised an eyebrow and nodded sagely. Jason levered to his feet and inhaled deeply of the pungent forest air. He met Santa's searching look. "For an hallucination, you're a convincing one." He glanced aside, thinking. "I'd like to believe you're real," he mused.

"That's my lad. I knew you had it in you." Santa beamed and pounded Jason's back.

"Now, my boy, a favour to ask. Dancer, here, has knocked his leg—could you have a look for us? Strangest thing you know, Dancer is the lightest and most graceful of the lot, can't imagine how he tagged himself like this. Coming off a roof in Mission, it was."

Jason and Santa bent over the injured Dancer's foreleg; the other reindeer pressed close.

"Can't see too well," muttered Jason, gently running his hand down the leg of the smallest reindeer.

Santa straightened. "Rudolph, my lad, come here and stand by Jason, if you will." The others made way for the large, radiant animal as he paced regally to Jason's side. He bent his stately head to Dancer's, then turned, gazing luminously at Jason. Jason, who'd always considered himself a practical, down-to-earth sort of guy, suppressed a shiver at the otherworldliness of that regard. He focused his attention on matters more easily understood.

"Nothing broken here—a simple abrasion. I've got some bandage material and Furacin ointment in my bag. That should do it."

As Jason fetched his bag he heard again the subliminal sound of the reindeers' melodious speech and Kris' rumbling voice in soothing reply.

"This bandage," Jason found himself addressing Dancer, "is like a Velcro fabric on one side—keeps the dressing neat." The reindeer sniffed at the material and

10

nodded. "Ok. Good." Jason blinked and stared a moment. "Right." He bent and applied a spiral wrap dressing to the dainty limb. "There," he looked up at Kris, "should be alright to remove it when you get back...home."

He grinned boyishly at Kris and the gathered reindeer. "I thought Dancer might approve the colour." The neat bandage was a bright Christmas red, to rival Santa's suspenders.

A lightness of heart and sense of joyful purpose was palpable in the air now. With much jingling of harness and crunching of hooves on frosty ruts, Kris rehitched his team. Grasping the leads, Kris leaned down and extended his hand to Jason.

"Remember what we spoke of tonight, dear boy."

Jason nodded. "I will. I promise."

Kris glanced at Jason's truck. "As for now, it seems there's a favour the lads and I can do for you."

***

Jason came to with a start. The road lay empty and shining pewter ahead of him; the dark evergreens sloughing the night wind. Somewhere, coyotes howled at a distant train. That spin had been a close call. If he'd gone in the ditch it could have finished the old truck not to mention himself. He slipped into low gear and cautiously released the clutch.

Christmas morning, Jason awoke feeling fresh in spite of the late night call to the clinic. Yvonne, who now called her "baby bump" a "baby balloon", reached awkwardly to lift the last present from near the base of their tree. She placed the small package in Jason's hands. It was wrapped in bright red foil, and directed simply, "To Jason".

She settled back to watch him open it. "Well? Who's it from?"

Jason shook his head. He tore at the red wrap. Inside was a hand-sized, heavy crystal globe containing a carved winter scene. A snowglobe? Shaking it, "snow" fell gently—raising the crystal to eye level created an illusion of vast horizons of forest and winter sky. Against the winter sky was an intricately carved red sled complete with Santa, and eight exquisitely detailed reindeer. The smallest of the reindeer looked not ahead like the others, but straight at Jason, the viewer, and sported a bright red bandage on his left front foreleg.

The End

Recipe for Santa's Favourite Hot Chocolate

3 T Hot Chocolate Mix (Instant)

1 T Chocolate Syrup

½ t Ground Cinnamon

1 pinch Chili Powder

¼ C Milk

¾ C Boiling Water

In large mug, mix the hot chocolate mix, chocolate syrup, cinnamon and chili powder.

Pour the milk. Add the boiling water and stir.

Chapter Two

CHRISTMAS RUNAWAY   *by Mimi Barbour*

Sara Hanson was miserable. What in the world had possessed her to give her young son Kai permission to spend Christmas holidays with his best friend's family in Hawaii? Three months ago when the topic came up, he'd worked on her. Not having the heart to refuse, she'd caved. Obviously, she hadn't thought about the fact that she'd be left alone on her favourite day of the year.

Blinding snow made driving almost impossible. She shouldn't have waited so long to start back home. But she couldn't leave Nanaimo without making sure that his plane had taken off safely and arrived the same way in Vancouver, then a stop at the mall for life-saving necessities such as chocolate and a favourite bottle of wine. Add a few more stops, like dinner at her favourite Thai restaurant and a movie that should have made her laugh but didn't, and here she was driving home too late, and through weather that had deteriorated dreadfully. Ice formed in sheets on the roads as the thermometer dropped when night fell, and treacherous didn't begin to describe the conditions.

Thankful that Pegi, her Samoyed, had travelled with her, she turned to pet the whining animal. "Don't worry girl. We'll be fine on our own. Kai deserves to be with his friends for Christmas. You and I'll celebrate with a spinster party just as soon as we get back to our cozy fireplace. We're not too far now, and as long as I go slow, we'll get there."

Her pet still seemed agitated, and so Sara opened the passenger window a little, knowing how much her dog liked to stick her nose out and breathe in some fresh air.

The radio had been acting up for the last few miles and finally became so distorted she shut it off. A loud cracking noise had her squinting through the blinding snow to see if a problem lay ahead on the road. She couldn't see anything but huge flakes of never-ending snow. All of a sudden the street lamps flickered and went out leaving the highway totally black. Only her headlights gave light and some solace, as they filtered through the mesmerizing curtain of blinding white.

Unexpectedly, Pegi lunged at the passenger door next to her and barked. Without thinking, Sara stepped hard on the brake, which forced the car to fishtail. Like an aircraft on takeoff, it glided to one side of the road, and overcompensating the turn made the vehicle head straight to the other side and into the ditch.

"Pegi? What in the world is wrong with you, girl? Stop that noise. Look what you made me do." She wailed the words and grabbed for the dog's collar at the same time. "Settle down."

But the agitated animal continued her uproar. She seemed to sense that the only way out was on Sara's side. Climbing on her lap, sharp toes digging in, whining and quivering, she demanded to be let out.

"Wait till we get home. Pegi, stop this nonsense." She tried to push the huge, furry white monster back over to her side of the car, but to no avail.

Pegi wouldn't let up, and instead, became even more forceful.

"Fine. I'll open the door, but you can't run off. You hear me? Stay close." Sara grabbed her gloves and the flashlight she always carried under her seat and shut the car off. She left the lights on as a safety precaution, and released the latch only to have the weight of the big animal wrench the door from her hand. It swung open, and in a flash, the distraught, barking dog sailed out and disappeared. Frustrated, Sara stepped out of the car only to land on her backside. "Damn ice," she muttered, as she carefully got to her feet only to see her dog bounding through the snow behind them. "That's it, you dumb beast. Ever heard of the pound where they stick crazy canines in cages and feed them dried veggies pellets?"

Commands for the dog to 'get back here right now' got no response. Now I'll have to go and get her, she thought. Bloody hell! That's all I need — fall face first in a snowbank and get my feet soaked chasing an untrained, bratty pet. "Arrggg!"

The barking plus the trampled snow gave Sara an indication of her pet's direction. Sputtering and swearing divested a little of her rising ire and lowered her blood pressure somewhat, but to say she felt annoyance eating into her stomach lining would be putting it mildly.

The staccato yelping continued and rose to frenzied proportions. Sara started into the direction the noise came from. She knew she couldn't leave her big baby out in the night alone.

Chiding whatever impulse made her choose to wear her fashionable high-heeled boots over the practical ones she usually preferred had her shaking her head. She put on her gloves, powered her flashlight, and started in the direction of her dog's cries.

Wet, sticky snow had built up over a foot high on the roads, in some places even higher, and was much worse when she headed for the side. The trees were thick and the gullies deep with lots of brush under the snow to trip her up. In her anxiety, the first stump she fell over only earned a grunt and a groan, but the next few made her let loose with some of her more colourful cusses. Only her determination to beat her dog senseless kept her going. Like that was going to happen. Pegi, the fanciful canine that believed she was human and had rights to the end of her mistress' bed was the most spoilt animal in the world. The fear that her pet might be in trouble was what drove Sara on.

Rocks barred her way, branches ripped at her legs, while her indulgent, twelve-dollar pair of silk stockings became their victim. To stop never entered her mind. Her beloved's begging cries and her own stubborn streak forced her onward.

Finally, her flashlight beamed on the silly, crazed mutt and instead of returning to her mistress when ordered, the creature led her further into the woods. Just when Sara decided not to play this insane game any longer, Pegi ran up to a dark mass leaning against a tree. It was then she saw movement and heard the murmur of a girl's voice.

Sara rushed forward to drop to her knees beside the quivering youngster. Shushing the distraught dog, she knelt down and shone her flashlight into the face of a frightened teen. "My God! Are you okay, sweetheart?" Brushing the wind-blown hair away from the face of the frightened girl, she added. "Don't be afraid. Pegi's big, but gentle as a lamb. She's barking because she's worried about you."

"I can't believe you've come. I gave up hope." The young voice broke, and Sara watched as the girl bit her lip. Amazed by her control, Sara waited. "Your dog woke me and keeps pushing at me to get up, but I've hurt my ankle, and I can't. It's swollen and won't take my weight." Now sobbing, the youngster's fear came through loud and clear.

Once Sara was able to make out the girl's features, she guessed she was probably twelve or somewhere around that age. The bluish tinge to her lips, and her shivering, told Sara that hypothermia had started to set in, and getting her back to the car became her top priority.

"Look sweetheart, I need you to stay with me. Don't pass out again. I'm going to piggyback you to my car on the highway, and we'll get you warmed up. Okay? Now tell me what you're doing in these bushes and so far off the highway." She boosted the girl up and gave her the light so she could shine it in front of them. Lifting her the same way she'd carried Kai to bed before he got too old, she balanced the weight on her back and held on to the arms around her neck.

"I got angry at my dad and ran away. I stayed off the highway so he couldn't find me. Once the snow started, I decided to try and get back to the road, but I tripped over a tree and must have hit my head. I think I passed out for a while. When I came to, I couldn't remember which way to go. It was dark and I couldn't see. My foot hurt so much, that I...I." Her sobs made understanding her words impossible.

"Don't cry, honey. I've got you now, and you're going to be fine. Oops…" By paying attention to the child, and not where she headed, Sara smashed into a rock and took a good hit to her knee. A strong back and good muscle tone kept her from dropping her passenger and going down altogether, but her blasted heels kept giving way so her ankles wobbled back and forth like a kid in her first pair of skates. "My name is Sara Hanson and this mutt is my dog Pegi. What's your name?" Sara knew she had to keep the girl talking.

"I'm Amy Watson. My dad is the new director for the Oceanside Clinic. He's also a doctor."

"We need doctors in this community, so I'm very glad to welcome you both. Look, you can see the headlights which means we're almost there. Hopefully we'll have cell phone access, but out here it's not great at the best of times. And with this storm, who knows?" Slithering and sliding, bent almost in half, and often leaning on her oversized dog, after a good fifteen minutes, Sara finally got them to where the car sat lopsided in the ditch.

Amy slipped off Sara's back and balanced on her good foot, using the car as a leaning post. It took precious moments to pry open the back door, but finally the latch gave, and she helped Amy slide onto the car. "Lay back, honey. Put your feet up on the seat. That's good." It took only moments to get herself and Pegi into the front and to start the engine so the heater blasted warm air. Once settled, she removed her coat and took off the fuzzy sweater underneath and piled both on Amy whose teeth chattered incessantly.

Despite the chapped lips and reddened cheeks, Sara could see the girl was a beauty.

Auburn hair, naturally curly, had escaped from a ponytail and formed tiny ringlets around her pretty face, highlighting her drenched emerald eyes. Thank goodness her slender body hadn't weighed overly much, or Sara wouldn't have been able to carry her.

"Thank you. Your sweater feels warm. I can't stop shaking. Wow, I never really understood how cold—cold could be." Amy's chattering sounded weird with her teeth clicking continuously.

Agile from years of yoga, Sara maneuvered herself past the floor console and into the back seat where she checked Amy's swollen leg. "Can you move your foot? I think it's best to leave the boot on. It's keeping the leg from swelling worse." Not being great at first aid, Sara had always relied on her nursing neighbour to bandage Kai's scrapes and wounds most active boys suffered. "I wish your father was here."

Even though the words "me too" were whispered, Sara heard them distinctly. "Dad's going to kill me when I get home. He's so busy with his new job; he hasn't had time for me at all. I miss my friends in Vancouver so much, and I only wanted to spend a few days with them over the holidays, but he refused to consider it. Said he had no time to bring me there. Like I couldn't take the ferry myself. Treated me like a kid, and freaked out when I pushed him on it. You know, I've tried to understand about his work, really I have. But he doesn't care that my life is over. That I have no friends here. That I'm miserable." Tears gushed and streamed, drenching her cheeks and pouting lips.

Immune to displays of self-pity, Sara added. "So to fix him, you ran away in a snowstorm to hide in the woods. Where you could have died rather than sit the foolish man down, explain your feelings, and talk to him like an adult."

"He doesn't listen."

"Do you talk? Or scream and pout?"

The silence was telling. "I'm a brat, aren't I? I'm so sorry." She held her hand toward Sara, pleading for comfort, and Sara could no more ignore the gesture than stop the hug that followed. Pegi, bounding over to land on top of them, broke up the moment and had them laughing. "Get into the front Pegi. Amy's fine now." Sara smoothed the girl's long straggly hair from her face and kissed her cheek. "She could never stand it when my son and I got into a battle either. From the first sign of tears, she'd do anything to stop the war." Sara reached into her pants pocket and pulled out her cell phone. "I need to call for help. I haven't seen anyone else on the road since we got here."

The bars pointed to a full battery, but the words 'No Service' illustrated clearly they were out of luck. Darn it! Sara thought through her options and decided she had no choice.

"Amy, we can't keep the car going, or we'll run out of gas. We're stuck too deep in the snow for me to drive out, and my house is too far for me to carry you. Our only hope is for me to try and find a signal further up the road and call a neighbour who doesn't live too far away. He has a four-wheel drive vehicle and would come and get us. Look, there's a straight stretch past the curve up ahead. I'll try there. Give me your father's number so I can add it into my address book and I'll call him also." She carefully copied the numbers and then redressed in her coat and gloves. Before she left the vehicle she reached into the bag on the floor by the front seat and pulled out a fancy parcel. "In the meantime, here's a huge bar of chocolate for you to nibble. I'll be back as soon as I've reached someone."

She pulled on her headlights, pushed the heavy door with all her might to dislodge the recent snow, and heaved herself out. "No Pegi. You stay and keep Amy company." With a shove on the animal's chest to push her back, she slammed the door, then slid and fumbled her way to where she surmised the road lay. So much snow had fallen in the last twenty minutes that without the faint treads from her tires, she'd never have found the highway. Her skewered headlights illuminated the curve sign, and using baby steps, she glided in that direction. Holding her phone in front of her, Sara prayed for a change.

She stopped to get her bearings, and what she saw made her shudder. Wind, that earlier was quite light, had picked up to almost gale force. Banks of snow had formed everywhere, and the blizzard conditions made walking so treacherous, she had no idea how she stayed upright. Her hair whipped out from under the turned-up hood on her coat and slapped at her cheeks and eyes forcing tears to overflow, all but blinding her.

How could a perfectly ordinary day turn out so badly? Here she was stuck in a ditch in one of the nastiest snowstorms she'd ever seen, with an injured runaway in her car, and if she couldn't get her phone to work, no way to get help. Things couldn't get much worse.

Blaringly loud, the honking horn made her spin around and instinctively dive for where she hoped lay the edge of the road, but not before seeing the driver

22

fight the wheel of an SUV gone loco. The crash, buffeted by so much snow, didn't sound half as loud as she expected. Dazed, and lying on her side, she watched the front end of the vehicle plough through the drifts of soft snow, dip into a gully, and became wedged, looking like a one of those chauvinist joke videos they send over the internet depicting women drivers.

Stunned, she lay there, gathering her scattered wits and questioning the higher power about his sense of humour.

Rage rumbled through the voice of the man who limped over to drag her from the ditch. "What the hell is wrong with you lady? Are you nuts, standing in the middle of the road?"

Knowing from many arguments with her son that the defensive role didn't work, she quickly chose the offensive. "Me? The speed you were driving, in these conditions, you could have killed me."

"Unsurprisingly, the urge is still there." His droll tone hinted at temper reined in, but just.

Sara, still clutching her flashlight, shone it up into his face and saw a man looming over her who clearly had a great deal on his mind. Lurking behind the visible anger, she sensed worry and what looked like fear. That alone helped her to forgive his rotten attitude.

In a placating manner that was so Sara, her hand reached out to touch his arm. "Look, I'm fine, and I'm sorry for scaring you. But I have an emergency. My car is stuck in a snowdrift around that bend, and I couldn't get phone service there. Useless old phone that it is. I hoped that if I came to the straight stretch, I might get a signal. I guess I became so engrossed, I didn't even notice your headlights." For a moment, she didn't think he'd accept her explanation. The man ignored her and repeatedly ran his hands through his wind-blown hair, his agitation obvious. Then, as her words registered, he grabbed her arms, she supposed to shut her up, and interrupted in a voice that normally she'd never have put up with.

"What kind of an emergency? Late for a party?" His sarcasm grated, but before she could volley back, he continued, his voice breaking with emotion. "I have a thirteen-year-old, runaway daughter who could be roaming these woods. The silly twit has no survival skills of any sort for this kind of weath —"

"Amy Watson is your daughter? Oh my goodness, she's my emergency also. My dog found her in the bush, and we've brought her to the car, but I'm scared she's in the first stages of hypothermia. I was desperate to get help before I run out of gas. She needs to be indoors."

The chauvinistic brute disappeared, replaced instantly by a frightened father who unthinkingly lowered his forehead to touch hers in a way that tore the heart right out of her. A sucker for any kind of male emotion, Sara wrapped an arm around the stranger and held on for a few seconds. Her voice gentled. "She's fine, just a swollen ankle on top of being frightened and cold. Come with me, I'll show you."

The first step she took would have landed her on her fanny without his assistance. "Dear Lord! You are a menace, aren't you? Look! Don't move for a minute until I turn off my car and get my medical bag. Then I'll help you."

24

As she waited, she sifted through the pithy responses she should have made after his smart-ass remark. Instead, she said nothing and shone the flashlight to help him see his way better. On his return, she couldn't help but notice how young he appeared and — well — dark. From his full eyebrows and longish hair, to his eyes and his heavy jacket, and when she added his personality into the mix, it looked to be a long night.

Sara, aware her eyes were a dead giveaway to her thoughts, looked away. "I hope Amy isn't scared with me being gone so long. She was pretty upset by the time I found her."

"Lately she's become emotional over every little thing. Trust me, I know."

"It's called puberty. As a doctor, I'm sure you're aware of the phenomenon. It happens to teenage girls." Her snippy tone came out without any thought of how it would sound to a virtual stranger. Between her and Kai, they tended to 'dis' each other, as he called it, 'push buttons' to her way of thinking, and her response had come automatically.

His head swivelled, and he eyeballed her innocent expression before answering. "I'm an administrator, not a practising MD. But I do know what that means. And, I've given her a lot of slack. Obviously too much, since she thought she could pull off a stupid stunt like she did today."

"I think she's sorry for running away. She's been frightened, and that in itself is a huge lesson." Involved in the conversation and not paying attention to her next step, Sara, arms windmilling, instinctively grabbed at the person nearest to stop her imminent fall. Rather than stop herself from landing on her backside, she hauled him down with her.

"Lady, you're a hazard. It should be mandatory every time you leave your house for you to strap on a blinking yellow light." She noticed he'd taken the brunt of their misfortune by twisting, trying to save her at the last minute.

The flashlight in her hand was caught between their two bodies and illuminated their faces. At the same moment, they both stopped trying to push away from each other. Instead their gazes caught and held. Shivers broke out all over her body, which had nothing to do with the fact that she lay partially buried in a foot of snow, but all to do with a stranger's arms cradling her. His eyes—not black at all—replicated her all-time favourite ring, one she'd cherished for years, a brilliant aquamarine.

Neither of them moved for what seemed like forever, but was in fact probably only a few seconds. In that time, she felt as if he'd seen into her very soul with a disconcerting gaze that had her stomach flip-flopping and her breath catching in her throat.

Lordy, lordy, she thought, giddy as a young girl. He's rather smashing. His raised eyebrow finally caught her attention, stopped her ogling, and brought her back to earth.

"Sorry! Look, the car's just there, you can see the headlights." She nodded towards the side of the road where a faint glow sent strange shadow images into the trees. Then she breathed a sigh of relief when he lifted her off of him, and with one smooth move, rolled to his feet. Like any gentleman, once he stood, he reached down to help her up.

She ignored his outstretched hand, knowing with her luck, she'd have another blunder. Then he'd really have something to tease her about. And she was right. Not only did her feet slide out from under her, but if he hadn't thought quickly and one-armed her against his body, she'd have landed once again on her backside.

Horrified, she tried to push his hands away.

"Oh for heaven's sake." He wrapped his free arm around her and all but carried her to the car. Once there, he opened the front door and shoved her in like a victim in a kidnapping. Pegi, not liking this at all, lunged forward, warning the stranger with a menacing growl.

"Stop, Pegi! Don't bite him—yet. But keep that thought in case I change my mind." Sara didn't care if he heard her loudly whispered words.

Amy sat forward. "Sara, are you alright. I got worri... Daddy?" Her father had opened the back door, slid her feet over, and pushed his way inside. "You came to find me?"

"You sound surprised." The brusque tone in his voice didn't cover the relief that Sara heard loud and clear.

"I am. I didn't think I was important enough for you to leave your office for so long."

"You didn't think at all. Why would I give anyone else the joy of wringing your neck? As your father, I relish the privilege."

Sara couldn't hold back another minute. "Stop it you two. Squabbling like a couple of kids. You've devastated your frantic father, Amy. Of course he's searched for you and in this horrible weather." Then she pointed her gloved finger toward the man whose name she still didn't know and hesitated. "What's your name?"

"Mr. Watso—"

"Dad!"

"Jack. And I wasn't quite that frantic since I knew my little girl has a sharp head on her shoulders, and in normal circumstances, could look after herself very well."

"Really, Dad? Do you really believe that? Don't kid around, okay? I pulled a dumb move and could have been seriously in trouble if Pegi hadn't found me." The sob that escaped had both the man and the dog moving towards the youngster.

Just in time, Sara grabbed the collar to keep her pet in the front seat and watched as the man scooped his daughter onto his lap and hugged her with a moan breaking his restraint. "You scared me, kiddo. This time you really had me worried. Don't ever take off like that again."

The crying teen buried her face, and her arms clung to his neck as she sobbed brokenheartedly. "I was just so lonely. And it's Christmas. And my friends are all together without me. A-and you didn't care."

"What can I say? I'm an unthinking jerk. There were so many loose ends at the office, and I'd decided if I could finish them all early, we could have the rest of today and tomorrow to celebrate. But then everything fell apart..." He stopped when he heard her loud sigh. "You're right. Same old excuses. I'm really sorry, baby. No more work. I promise."

"I'm sorry to have worried you." The youngster's voice wobbled, but her sincerity rang true.

"I guess I understand how important your job is right now while you're setting everything up. You explained it to me—ad nauseam—a-and I know I promised to cut you some slack. It's just that the new house isn't home to me. And not having anyone around was driving me crazy. I hate spending all day alone. Hold it!" Her voice rose shrilly. "Before you remind me that I have all the toys other kids would love to have, it's—"

"No, I'll never say that again. While I drove around looking for you, I realized something radically awesome." Sara watched in the rear-view mirror as the teen smacked her father's arm in the way young girls do when they're being teased. "It dawned on me that I would hate to be treated like I was nothing but a hindrance. Especially since it isn't true. You alone colour my world, little girl. You always have. Without you everything would be—hmmm—yucky grey!"

"Awww, Dad." Sniffs and hugs followed. Soon, in a little girl voice, Amy continued. "And now, because of me, we're all stuck in a snowstorm, huddled in a cold car on Christmas Eve."

Feeling she'd given the father and daughter sufficient time to make up, Sara butted in. "Couldn't help but overhear, and I just want you to know that we don't have to remain in the car. If your dad feels up to carrying you, my house is within walking distance. Wanna go for it?"

"Can we? Cool!" Instinctively, Amy flung her hand toward Sara and smiled when it was taken and held for a moment.

Without thought, before letting it go, Sara kissed the back gently. Jack's startled gaze caught hers. Why she blushed, she'd never know. Something in his look made her lower her eyes and pretend an interest in her furry pet.

"Did Sara tell you I hurt my ankle, Dad? I can't put any weight on it."

"Right, I brought my bag with me. Let's take a look."

Sarah added without turning around. "We didn't take her boot off because I thought the tightness of the leather would give the same support as a tensor bandage." Hoping she hadn't made a mistake, she glanced back to see if his face showed any distain or anger.

His answer made her relax. "You're probably right. Can you wait until we get to Sara's house, Amy? Then I'll take it off and look at the damage."

"Sure. No problem. Except I can't put any weight on it at all. Sara had to piggyback me to the car." Amy grinned with affection, and without hesitation Sara grinned back.

"You're lucky I didn't put us both in the snowbank with these silly boots I'm wearing."

"For some women, it's all about being modern and looking good rather than practicality." Jack's stiff voice caught both her and Amy's stare.

"You're kidding, right?" Sara couldn't stop from challenging his remark. "I'm wearing these silly boots because it was a sad day for me, and I wanted to dress frivolously for once to help cheer myself. I took my son to the airport and thought I'd be spending the night alone, so... Hold it! What time is it??" Her voice broke, the worry coming through loud and clear.

Without hesitation, Jack answered. "Close to seven. Is there a problem?"

"Yes. Kai, my son, promised to Skype me at seven-thirty my time, and he'll be frantic if I'm not there to answer. He knows nothing would keep me from hearing how his trip went. We must leave now."

"Yes, okay. Is it very far?"

"About a quarter of a mile. I knew I couldn't carry Amy myself, but I'm sure for you it won't be too difficult. There are heavy trees along the sides of the road, might block some of the snow. Make it easier to traverse, but it'll still be quite a trek."

"Then let's get started." Jack helped Amy to get ready. He took his scarf off his own neck and solicitously wrapped it around her head, tucking it into her jacket as if she were a child. He was unaware that Sara watched until she sighed.

"What?"

"Nothing. Are we ready? I'll leave the car lights on. As weak as they are, they'll help somewhat. The turn-off is the second on the right, and the lane goes all the way to the beach. I just had the road repaired and made ready for the winter. Should help some."

The next while was something Sara would never forget. Between her windmilling falls, Jack's muttering each time he stopped to assist, and him dropping Amy when Sara would unwittingly upend him, their sombre plodding turned into hilarious antics. At least for her and Amy. Jack—not so much. But the occasional grin did break through, and all in all, he went along with their foolishness good-naturedly.

By the time they reached her front door, not only were they exhausted frozen snowpeople, but they needed to get out of their wet clothes and put something hot into their cold bodies. While Jack used his cell phone to informed the local police that there were two vehicles in the ditch but the occupants were safe, Sara had the furnace turned up, the fireplace on and the overly decorated living room glowing like the cover of an old-fashioned Christmas card. Angels and reindeer, her favourite decorations, were placed haphazardly around the room, and the huge blue spruce decorated in a traditional way gave off the most wonderful smell of the season. An overabundance of fanciful ornaments, sparkling glitter and tinsel saved from years gone by caught one's eye, but it did represent Christmas. Or so Sara imagined.

"I'll get Amy something to change into," Sara played hostess. "Jack, Kai's room is the first up the stairs on your right. Check his closet and see if there's anything that'll fit you. You're a big man, but then he's a big boy and wears a lot of his clothes baggy so you might luck out."

"Yes ma'am." Jack stomped the snow from caked boots and shrugged off his coat. Amy saw his well-groomed suit, soaked from the knees down, and loved the fact that his once perfect tie was wrinkled and hung loosened around his neck.

In no time, everyone spiffed up in sweats, met in the kitchen where Sara began setting out the remains of the huge Christmas dinner she'd shared with Kai the day before. Over the large, wooden, county-styled table, she spread platters of turkey, ham, cabbage rolls, salad and on and on, then plunked three plates with cutlery down and waved her hands for them to dig in. Before sitting down, she filled an extra plate for Pegi who strangely ignored the food.

Sara, thinking it odd since her dog normally wolfed down her dinner, didn't force her but instead wiped her down and then busied herself with other chores.

"Fill your plates and I'll heat them up in the microwave," she said, with a friendly slap on Amy's hand for picking at the meat without a fork.

As soon as they were all loaded with food and drinks, wine for her and Jack, and a wine goblet filled with ginger-ale for Amy, they began their meal. Sara grabbed the fancy candles that she and Kai had used and relit them to give a festive air to their holiday feast.

Pegi hovered close to Sara, not her usual habit, until Sara with a glare and a finger pointing at the mat near the back door where the dog's supper waited, forced the dog to obey without a word spoken. The large white fur-ball crept to the corner and whined.

"Sara, I love your Pegi. She's wonderful." Amy sighed and then glared at her dad.

"Noted and filed, dear daughter. When we're settled, we'll look into getting a pet. I was thinking a turtle might be fun." Jack winked at Sara, but Amy didn't notice.

"Da-d! Give me a break!" The whine was well practised. So was the pout.

Sara winked back at Jack and added. "I have a really small collar you can use to take it for a walk, Amy. Think of all the attention you'll get at the beach in the summer."

Amy's glance swivelled between her father and Sara and then she smiled. "You're kidding, right?"

Jack answered before Sara. "You think so?" Then he motioned for Amy to turn towards him. "Here, give me your foot. I see you got the boot off between the two of you. Was it very painful?"

Amy lifted her leg onto his knee. "Sara wiggled it and worked it off. It didn't hurt too much. I can even put a bit of weight on it now."

After he prodded and poked, he nodded. "Good. Keep it up as much as possible to keep the swelling down. Maybe an ice pack would help also."

Sara jerked and dropped the knife she held while cutting into a loaf of homemade bread, and quickly turned towards the large refrigerator behind her. "I meant to give her one and forgot."

Feeling inadequate, Sara organized the pack and handed it over without looking at Jack. As he took the ice, he grasped her hand and used this to force her to look at him. The softness in his eyes surprised and pleased her at first. Then tingles started from where their hands linked, ran up her arm straight to her heart, and exploded into sensations that had her catching her breath. Reflexes kicked in, and she snatched her hand back. What in the world? From under her eyelashes, she noticed him shake his own hand before clenching and hiding it under the table.

Just then the computer let her know that Kai had made his promised call. She moved to where it sat at a workstation on the side of the kitchen and opened the page. At first glance, she noted his annoyance. Before she could speak, he blurted out in his forthright manner.

"Where were you Mom? This is the third time I've tried to get through. I was worried."

"Now you know how it fee —"

"Not funny Mom. I was really worried."

"No, you're right. I'm sorry, Kai. There was a snowstorm on the way home, and I ran into a slight problem."

"Oh man! You mean you hit someone?"

"Don't take me so literally. No I didn't hit someone, I sort of ran off the road when I stopped to help a young—" Busted!

"Don't tell me you picked up a hitchhiker. Mom, that's crazy dangerous."

Sara felt the other two people in her kitchen trying not to listen as they helped themselves to the food she'd put out for their benefit, but it's impossible to shut off your ears. Time to change the subject.

"Well it all turned out fine. Tell me how your trip went and about Hawaii? Is it really beautiful?" She smiled at the screen and saw Kai swallow and look uncomfortable. What's up with that?

"I missed you, Ma. You should be here with me. It's not right I left you alone and over Christmas. It ate away at me all the way here. I'm a spoiled brat and a rotten son."

"You want me to make you feel better, dontcha?" She giggled and watched his expression lighten.

"Yeah." He half grinned, his endearing dimple creasing his cheek, but only on the one side. Blonde waves framed his face, and his father's blue eyes beamed at her with affection.

The expression he wore reminded her of when he was little, had done something naughty and needed her forgiveness before he could let it go. His guilt tolerance level was non-existent.

All of a sudden, he stiffened and his gaze became guarded. "Who's the chick there with you?"

She turned to see that Amy had stood, intending to go over to Pegi who seemed to be choking on something.

"It's a long story. Let's just say Pegi found her lost in a snowstorm, and she's visiting with me for a while."

"Lost in a snowstorm? Harsh!"

Just then Jack stood, watching to see if the dog would accept Amy's ministrations.

Kai's tone changed, hardened. "Who's the Dude?" Sitting alert now, he looked to be the man he would one day become; ready to take on the world for those he loved.

"I'm the chick's dad." Sara hadn't realized that Jack had moved to stand behind her.

She glared a warning at Jack and said. "Kai, this is Jack Watson. He's the Director for the new medical clinic in Parksville. He and his daughter are my guests tonight because of the storm."

Her son's eyes narrowed. His attitude cool, but not over the line. "Hi, Mr. Watson."

Sara, proud of her son's manners, nodded her approval. Suddenly, strange noises from the corner alerted Sara that her pet seemed to be in difficulties, and so she quickly added.

"Would you like to meet Amy? Since she's new to the area, I'm sure she'd be pleased to meet someone her own age." Sara turned and waved at Amy, then smiled as she shyly nodded and then hobbled over.

"Kai this is Amy Watson. She hurt her ankle earlier, and Pegi and I helped her." Sara had to get to her dog, who she knew was in extreme difficulties in the corner. "Be nice, both of you." She helped Amy to sit and quickly went over to where Jack spoke soothingly to her distressed pet.

Seeing her coming, Pegi tried to stand, but the animal's heaving and gagging made it difficult. With Sara's help, the frightened dog finally staggered to her feet and instantly became violently sick.

"Mom, what's going on?" Kai had seen the commotion long enough to know his best friend was in trouble.

Sara called over from where she stood, patting the retching canine. "It's crazy, but she's acting the same way she did when she broke into my Purdy's chocolate stash last year. Remember how sick she was?"

"Oh, no," Amy groaned. "It's my fault then. When you left me the big chocolate bar, I shared it with her. She lapped it up. I'm sorry, Sara, I didn't know it would make her sick." She hid her red face in her hands, but not before Kai saw the glistening of tears.

He spoke before Sara. "Don't worry, Amy. Last time it happened the vet said she'd puk...ahh expel the stuff and be fine, and she was. Mind you she was sicker'na dog for a couple hours." His cheeky grin did the trick, and Amy visibly relaxed.

Sara called over her shoulder. "It's my fault too, honey. I didn't warn you not to give her any. She's such a beggar, I should have known better."

Prone, thoroughly exhausted, Pegi lay with her head in Sara's lap. While she massaged and petted the weak animal, she talked nonsense in a tone filled with love. To Sara's amazement, Jack had miraculously cleaned away the evidence of the animal's sickness without having spoken a word. Impressed that a man would help out in such a way, she sent him a loving glance without realizing how potent. Then wondered why he stopped in his tracks.

He moved closer and caressed her hair. He said, his voice low, "I'm so sorry about this Sara. I know Amy feels terrible about hurting Pegi. But I'm sure now that most of the toxins are out of her system, she'll begin to recover." Jack watched as Pegi struggled to her feet, then stumbled and righted herself once again. "She wants to go out. I'll let her, shall I? She'll probably be more comfortable in the cool air."

"Yes, please." Sara tidied the mat and decided to return to her son who was chatting away to his new friend.

She stopped to eavesdrop — the right of every mother with a teenage child — and couldn't help but overhear the conversation.

Kai's voice, more enthusiastic than at any time when he talked with her, sounded strangely deep and far too manly to belong to her fifteen-year-old.

"Amy, girl, you'll like the school. The kids rule!"

Sara started and had to bite her lip. Her husband, Kai's father, always referred to her in that endearing way, Sara girl, and to hear Kai use the same phrase made her heart melt.

Amy, much cheerier now, answered. "Are there lots of activities? I've always been involved in sports. I play soccer and ice hockey."

"You do? Dope! I play hockey too. What position?"

"Goalie."

"No way! Me, too. The net's the place to be."

"Yeah? I know what you mean." Amy had lost all her reticence. Now relaxed in the chair, her finger twirling her long strands of curls, her face alive with interest, she looked much different from the unhappy girl Sara had met earlier.

Sara hated to interrupt, but she really wanted to know how Kai had fared with his hosts and the trip. She moved to lean over Amy whose green eyes sparkled up at her alive and full of glee. "Kai, I hate to interrupt, but I want to know the telephone number to the hotel and the number to your room in case I have to get in touch with you."

"Sure mom. I'll e-mail you all that stuff right after I finish talking with Amy." The no nonsense tone to his voice made her understand that her son was growing up and putting down an ultimatum. Wisely, she backed off. "Awesome!" She grinned while he groaned. "Merry Christmas, my guy. I'll talk with you tomorrow. Have fun there and be good." She blew him a kiss.

"Backatcha Mom. You be good too, and Merry Christmas." His innocent look didn't fool her at all. There was a message meant for her from the cheeky devil.

Jack, waiting in the background, fluffed his daughter's hair as he passed. "A few more minutes, Brat, then say goodbye. Right?"

"Sure, Dad."

Knowing the kitchen needed to be cleared, Sara turned to go back into the room only to stop dead in her tracks. "You've put away the dishes? Are you for real?"

"Amy's mom left us years ago. There's only me to do these chores at home. Me, and Amy, who's classic in getting out of having to help in the kitchen. Considering she's only thirteen, you wouldn't believe her excuses."

"I bet Kai's are more imaginative. An allergy to soap and we have a dish washer."

"The stoneware is too heavy. She can't carry more than one plate at a time."

"Why do we have to wash everything, every night when it's just getting used again tomorrow? Couldn't we just wipe things off with our napkins and leave them on the table."

"Okay, that's just plain lazy."

"Ya think? He'll spend an hour or more polishing his ATV's hubcaps but...?" Her shrug spoke a thousand words.

Jack shrugged. "Gotta admit, in the big scheme, hubcaps are important..."

Her glare stopped him. "It's a man thing."

By this time, they each had a full glass of wine and were sitting together on the living room couch in front of the fire. She tapped her glass against his and shyly smiled. His searching look threw her until he smiled in return. He placed his arm around the back of the sofa and breathed deeply. "This is a wonderful room. You must love sitting here in the evening."

"I do. Except most times, I'm alone." As soon as the truthful words left her lips, she realized she'd spoken honestly and not with her usual reserve. Bloody hell! Her face felt hot. Whatever possessed her to be so open with a virtual stranger? She'd never admitted these feelings to anyone before. Embarrassment, and a huge amount of self-pride had kept the secret locked inside. She was a lonely soul and hated anyone to feel sorry for her. She snuck a peek at the man sitting next her.

He nodded as their eyes met. "I know what you mean. An empty room is still empty no matter how fancy the surroundings or decorations. It's most likely why I spend most of my evenings working in my home office." He picked up her hand, his so much bigger and stronger, hers so dainty next to his. His thumb rubbed her skin before he tightened his hold to draw her attention.

Understanding his aim to get her to look at him, she lifted her heavy eyelids and let him see her honest yearnings. It was like undressing in front of him, and she couldn't believe he'd earned her trust in such a short time. Never before had a man intrigued her this much. Her husband had won the love and affection of a young girl and had treated her like a princess until the day he'd died. But to this man, she was all woman. Her heart doubled its beat, while her tongue stayed glued to the top of her mouth. He was the first who'd reached her essence. Brought her sensuality to life. Made her feel ready to move forward.

Trembling, afraid, she tried to snatch her hand back. But he wouldn't let it go. "Oh no, Sara. It's too late to stop this now. We'll pursue this attraction to wherever it leads, and I have a feeling, it'll end up at forever."

"How can you say that? We've only just met."

"No we've only just found each other. We were destined to meet. I've been waiting for you all my life."

She couldn't look away. His eyes mesmerized. The warnings in her heart quieted. The trembling inside slowed and eased, while her soul whimpered in relief.

The yearnings faded.

He was here.

The End

Recipe for Mimi's Homemade Bread

In a large bowl add:
-4 cups of warm (not quite hot)
water
-1 tablespoon salt
-4 tablespoons sugar

Stir to dissolve.

Melt 4 tablespoons shortening
in Microwave and add to water

Add 2 cups of flour and stir into the water.

In next cup of flour, add 11/2 packages (1 full tablespoon) instant
yeast and stir it into the flour. Add to mixture.

From now on add 1 cup of flour at a time until the mixture is hard
to stir. Spoon it onto a floured counter and keep adding flour and
kneading it in until the dough forms a ball and the stickiness is
pretty well gone. It should be smooth and well kneaded. Takes
anywhere from 7-10 minutes.

Turn oven to a very low temp for a few minutes to warm it and then
warm the large bowl (with hot water) where the bread will rise.
Grease the bowl with some of the shortening and also grease the
top of the bread so no hard crusts form on the outside of the
dough.

Cover and let rise in the warm oven for 1 hour or until the dough
has doubled in size.

Then punch the dough down, put it on a floured surface and cut it
into 4 parts. Cover and let sit for 15 minutes.

Now, using a small amount of flour, shape the bread or buns to fit
into the pans. Cover and put in warm oven again to let rise for
another hour.

Cook at 350 for 25 to 30 minutes. Spread butter over top to soften
crust. Let sit on rack to cool and then enjoy!

Chapter Three

FLASH *by Clive Scarff*

Calvin was about as straight-laced as they come. Little about him was remarkable, certainly nothing was sensational. If he were any more mainstream he would stand alone. Of course, then, he would no longer be mainstream at all.

Mercredi, on the other hand, was curly-laced. That is, if one is to assume curly-laced is the opposite of straight-laced. She could be described as quirky, excitable, a firecracker, even a crackerjack. This could be due to her French Canadian heritage, the fact she was an accountant, or even more simply, a violent reaction to her parents naming her after a day in the week. Wednesday of all days.

Calvin and Mercredi had only been dating each other a few short weeks, but so far it had been going rather well. While their natures may have seemed incongruous, their likes were pretty much in line. Neither had to twist the other's arm to watch a movie, or a hockey game, take in a concert, go to the theatre. One could argue they were watchers, yet here they are, Christmas 2003, the subject of this story.

Vancouver Island is famous for having less rainfall than its relatively nearby neighbour, Vancouver. What they do not tell you is that is has about one day less rain, and it rains nearly every day except for July and August which are generally considered bad fishing months. And while this day was late December – Christmas Eve to be exact – it could be considered a bad fishing day. Some might even call it a drought, as it had not rained since the morning before. It was on this dry Christmas Eve that Calvin found himself pulling into the driveway at Mercredi's house, in the harbour town of Nanaimo. He had no sooner pulled in than the garage door in front of him opened automatically, and a black pick-up truck began to back out. Clearly in the way of the pick-up, Calvin appropriately backed out and decided to park on the street instead. This was his first mistake, and the beginning of a chain of events yet to unfold that evening.

Calvin had parked and was getting out of his car when he heard the sound of a fat fist on glass. Looking up, he saw an old woman in the window of the house he had just parked in front of. Holding a cup of coffee in one beefy mitt, with the other she again pounded on her living room window. Calvin's eyes met hers, and he could not help but think locking eyes with the devil himself would, somehow, be less intimidating. Her free hand then flicked from right to left, motioning him to move his car, much the same way an angry typist might flick the carriage return on an old Underwood typewriter. Somewhat dumbfounded, Calvin froze, not knowing what to do. Common sense dictated it was perfectly legal to park on the street where he had, but there was something that told him if this old woman ordered him to drink poisoned lemonade he would acquiesce. In the meantime, standing idiotically still seemed the order of the day.

The old woman moved to her front door, possessed. Suddenly it was open and she bellowed, "Move your damned car! They're coming back!"

Bewildered, and as if it mattered, Calvin meekly asked, "Who's coming back?"

"Move your damned car," she again yelled. "They're coming back to mow the grass and your bucket of rust is in the way. Move it! I want those dandelions –" and she said the next part with emphasis – "gone!"

Now, the fact it was late December and the grass had not grown in over two months seemed immaterial at this time. Calvin got back into his car to move it, and the old woman returned to her living room window to watch, making sure Calvin did as he was told. She took a big swig of coffee.

* * *

"I am so sorry, I should have warned you about her!" Mercredi blurted out as she opened the door for Calvin.

"The funny thing is I could have sworn I saw one of those 'You Are Entering A Nuclear Free Zone' signs when I pulled off the highway. I guess the zone ends at your house," Calvin retorted while taking off his jacket.

Mercredi's was a basement suite, and after closing the door and locking it behind Calvin she led him down a hallway to another door. She turned off the light for the hall they had just come through, opened the next door and flicked on a light in another hallway that led through what was obviously a shared laundry room. This led to another door; again Mercredi switched off the light, opened another door, reached in, and turned on another light. This one illuminated the front hall of Mercredi's suite.

"Boy, you have more halls than someone with a sore throat," Calvin offered.

Pointing to a door on the left Mercredi said, "You can throw your coat in there."

"Another hall?" Calvin asked.

"Spare room."

"The whole 'spare room' concept eludes me," Calvin declared. "It kind of implies that when the house was built they accidentally made too many rooms, and now there is one to spare. But it's not like you can loan it to someone like me who has too few rooms. For a room to be spare it should be somewhat portable, don't you think?"

Laughing, Mercredi replied honestly, "I guess I've never thought about it."

Calvin opened the door to what appeared to be a mausoleum for papers, books, files, DVDs, camping gear, and old kids' toys - he thought he saw a human limb in there too, but was not really sure. "Any chance I'll find that jacket again?" he asked, to no response. He followed Mercredi into the living room.

"I totally should have warned you about her; she is the nastiest woman on the street. Have a seat."

"We had an old lady on our street," Calvin offered, "who was so nasty the neighbours moved." He moved to the leather couch and sat down.

"Oh, I can see that happening," Mercredi responded.

"Ya," Calvin said, "but these were bikers. I can see your neighbour giving her a run for her money, though."

"Helga – that's the lady you just encountered – is always yelling at someone. Especially the people upstairs, telling them their dog is bothering her, to clean up their yard, that their dandelions are spreading to her house, all sorts of stuff."

"You're in trouble when someone with hubcaps for siding is telling you to clean up your yard," Calvin said.

"I think she's lonely," Mercredi explained compassionately. "No one ever comes to visit her."

"No wonder, if they did they'd have to park a mile away," Calvin claimed. "Wait 'til St. Nick tries to park on her roof. Are you not going to sit?"

"I am, but first I was going to offer you a drink. What can I get you?" Mercredi asked. "Beer? Wine?"

Calvin looked at his watch, "What time is the show?"

Moving to the kitchen Mercredi yelled back, "Not for a couple of hours."

"I guess a beer wouldn't kill me, thanks," Calvin responded.

Mercredi stuck her head back into the room. "Can or glass?" she asked.

"Glass, if you don't mind."

A moment later Mercredi returned, carrying two bottles of beer. She handed one to Calvin and sat down.

Awkwardly, Calvin inquired, "Did you forget the glass?"

"This is glass," Mercredi replied, holding up her bottle.

"Good point." Calvin smiled. He had been looking for someone who was low maintenance, and surely this would have to be a tick in the win column. He glanced around the room, and it seemed comfortable and perfect. There was stuff, but not too much stuff. There were girly things, but not too many girly things. There was a small white Christmas tree, lit with white lights and, unmistakable in the corner, was a man thing. It was approximately fifty-two inches wide, measured diagonally, with a flat screen. Tick.

"I quite like your name," Calvin declared.

"What? Mercredi?" she meekly asked.

"That is your name isn't it? Please don't tell me I've been calling you by the wrong day of the week since I've known you."

Smiling, Mercredi said, "I see you know a little French then."

"I can even tell you which day of the week," Calvin boasted, and then qualified, "if you give me seven guesses."

Mercredi made a face. "Well it's the most boring day of the week, if that helps. Every day of the week has something going for it, except Wednesday."

"That was going to be my seventh guess!" Calvin chirped. "But what's so bad about Wednesday?"

Mercredi took a swig of beer from her glass bottle. "Think about it, almost every day has an emotion attached to it, a positive function, even a nickname. Thursday is pub night, Friday is the end of the work week –"

"Thank God it's Friday," Calvin volunteered.

Mercredi continued, "Saturday is hockey night, Sunday is a day of rest and of religious significance."

"And makes me think of ice cream," Calvin added. "But Monday sucks."

"Yes, but at least it emits an emotion. And has its own song. Tuesday is cheap movie night. But Wednesday is just Wednesday. Boring old Wednesday, blah."

Calvin brightened. "Yes but it is known as –"

"Don't even go there, Mercredi insisted. And she did not appear to be joking.

Calvin could not resist continuing: "I'm just saying, during the work week when it gets to Wednesday people call that hu – "

"I know what they call it!" Mercredi interrupted. "And I said don't go there."

"But you can't really say it doesn't have a nickname when in actuality it does."

"But it's a stupid nickname!" Mercredi shouted.

"And as for eliciting emotion clearly – "

Again Mercredi cut Calvin off, "Can we change the subject please?"

"Of course," Calvin said, backing down. After a pause, he added, "I'm excited to see Ray Charles."

Completely recovered and a big smile leaping to her face, Mercredi said, "Oh, I am too! And I am so glad he is at the Port. It's an awesome theatre; it's a much smaller, more intimate venue."

"I've never been to the Port," Calvin said. "I am curious to see it."

Bubbly now, Mercredi added, "It's very nice, and we have great seats. Which reminds me, I must bring my camera."

"I don't think they allow cameras in most theatres," Calvin offered.

Mercredi clarified: "I always take my camera to concerts; they don't mind. Everyone does it."

"Well not everyone," Calvin said.

"Pretty much everyone," Mercredi replied.

"I don't."

"Well pretty much everyone but you, I guess. Why? Don't you have a camera?"

With a bemused smile Calvin explained, "Yes, I do have a camera. Or two. I just don't think performers want flash bulbs going off in their face when they are trying to perform."

Mercredi laughed. "Flash bulbs? How old are your cameras? Are they black and white?"

"You know what I mean," Calvin countered.

"Oh come on, get with the times," Mercredi said.

Calvin continued, "Plus I think they worry about you selling the pictures, or what you'll use them for."

"Oh they want you to take pictures, it's free promotion. Have you not seen YouTube? It launches careers."

"It didn't launch Ray Charles' career, but it's your call," Calvin declared. "Take your camera. But if they send you to jail I will deny knowing you."

"Ah, my white knight," Mercredi said as she smiled sweetly. "Another beer?"

"I better not," Calvin offered responsibly. "I'm driving; plus, when the camera police come after you I'd rather not smell of alcohol."

* * *

"Thank goodness for underground parking," Mercredi exclaimed as she got out of Calvin's now extremely wet car. The fishermen were happy again.

"Yeah, this is awesome the theatre has a parking garage. You can count on one hand the number of underground lots in Nanaimo," Calvin added.

"It's especially good at a theatre," Mercredi said, "where everyone is dressed up, and hair done. The last thing you want is to sit and watch a show soaking wet for two hours."

"That's the thing about snow. Everyone out here knocks it, but at least it doesn't soak you." Calvin reached into his pocket and retrieved some coins for the parking pay station as he continued, "Not to mention snow totally adds to the feel of Christmas. I miss it this time of year."

Receipt in hand, Calvin escorted Mercredi to a nearby door marked 'To Theatre'. Immediately they were delivered from the cold grey fluorescence of a puddled underground parking garage to the richly decorated vestibule of a new theatre at Christmas time. Christmas trees lined the lobby; no coloured Christmas lights, just white, a sudden substitute for the snow Calvin was mentioning he missed just moments ago. Christmas music was humming in the background, slightly above the modest din of a theatre lobby crowded with well-dressed patrons roaming around in organized confusion. Some were lined up at the coat check, eager to shed themselves of unwanted outerwear. Others lined up at the well adorned bar, yet others, already with drinks in hand, were mingling, chatting, in seasonally joyous anticipation of a Christmas concert by one of music's superstars.

It was not long before the peal of an inoffensive bell began, telling the patrons it was time to take their seats. As a crowd gathered at the opening of one

52

entrance to the theatre itself, Mercredi shoved her digital camera in Calvin's hand, "Here, take this."

"Why am I taking it?"

"Because you can put it in your pocket; they're more likely to search my handbag than your pocket."

"I'm confused, I thought we were going to see Ray Charles, not boarding a plane for Bangkok. Here, I don't want your camera."

"Shhh," Mercredi hushed Calvin. "They're looking, don't create a scene."

"Who's looking?"

"The ushers."

"Those little old ladies in white blouses?" Calvin inquired. "I thought they were a lawn bowling team. You claimed it was okay to bring cameras into theatres; everyone does it, you said."

"They do, but not out in the open, silly."

"No, that would be rude," Calvin conceded. "Look, if I have to put this in my pocket then you take my wallet. Two bulges in my pockets would be a dead giveaway, whereas a wallet in your handbag is not suspicious."

"Deal," Mercredi said, smiling and taking Calvin's wallet, which she then indeed placed in her handbag. The two proceeded past the team of ushers into the lavish theatre, without incident.

**

"Ladies and gentlemen, Mr. Ray Charles!" The words were barely spoken when Mercredi elbowed Calvin.

"Give it to me."

"Give what to you?" Calvin naively asked, in a hushed voice.

"The camera."

"He only just came on."

"Yes I know, it's Ray Charles."

"I know it's Ray Charles," Calvin explained. Persisting, "Give me the camera."

"Shhh," came an insistent and clearly annoyed voice from the row behind.

Pleading now, "Give it to me."

Calvin slouched down into his chair, as if to hide from the shusher behind, "I can't."

"Are you serious?" Mercredi demanded.

"Yes, I'm serious, I can't."

"Why not?" she asked.

"It's in my front pocket."

"So?" It was Mercredi's turn to be naïve.

"Because I would have to stand up to get it out and I'm not standing up in front of Ray Charles."

"Why not? He won't see you."

"Shhhhhhh!" This time the shushing came in triplicate.

Getting seriously impatient now, Mercredi's hand made a dart for Calvin's front pocket.

"Hey!"

"Shhhhhh!"

"What is the problem here?" The voice came from Calvin's right. It was eerily familiar. It was also just plain eerie. There, leaning in from the aisle, replete with standard issue usher's uniform, was Helga. The cranky lady from next door.

He did not, but it seemed as if Ray stopped playing, and the entire world was now focused on Row

H, seats 24 and 25. If he could have slouched down further in his seat he would have; Calvin mustered a feeble – and hushed – "There's no problem here."

Helga returned, "I can't hear you."

"That's because I'm trying to be quiet," Calvin explained.

"Well you weren't before," countered Helga. "What's that in your pocket?"

Now, half protruding from Calvin's front pocket was Mercredi's camera. Covering it with his hand, Calvin muttered, "It's just my wallet."

"Funny looking wallet."

"I got it in Japan," Calvin replied.

"Humph. Well keep it down."

"Yes ma'am," Calvin offered politely. As Helga walked away, Mercredi yanked her camera from Calvin's pocket. Calvin looked at her, but dared say nothing.

***

It was a good ten minutes before Mercredi actually used her photographic device; as if waiting ten minutes would fool the authorities. But Ray was singing Georgia and it had to be recorded, for posterity's sake and even if only visually. So out it came, and up she held it. "Don't," Calvin pleaded.

"Everyone else is," Mercredi countered.

"Where? I don't see anybody."

"That lady down there has been taking pictures the whole time with her cell phone, and there, that guy right there just took a picture," Mercredi said, pointing.

"The guy in black?"

"Yes, him, "Mercredi answered.

"The guy in black with the press badge?" Calvin inquired further.

"Shhh," came another voice from behind.

"Shhh," Mercredi added, and yes, she was shushing Calvin. "Do you want to get us in trouble again?"

"Oh no," Calvin responded, "I'll leave that to you."

Mercredi discreetly snapped a shot, then another, then another. She stopped to look at the pictures she had taken. "Too dark," she muttered.

"Oh no," Calvin muttered, to himself, as he slunk down further into his chair. The next shot lit up the entire row in front. Ray was not visible in it, but there was a wonderfully bright picture of the man-in-front's bald spot. Off went the flash again, and again.

"Stop!" Calvin pleaded, embarrassed.

"I need one good shot, and it's not working," Mercredi explained.

Calvin shot back: "Of course it's not. Ray's a hundred feet away and your flash goes twenty!"

"Good point, I'll make it brighter."

Again with the flash, and twice the intensity now. If the man in front had been wearing polyester he would have been in trouble. As it was, he probably should have been wearing sunscreen.

"That's enough," Calvin declared, snatching the camera away from Mercredi.

"Hey!" remarked Mercredi.

"I'll take that," said Helga.

There, in the aisle, standing tall (all 5'1" of her) was the chief-o'-ushers. "And you can come with me," she added.

"Who?" asked Calvin.

"You," came the response. "And don't make me get help."

"But – "

"Help!" Helga then flashed her mini flashlight six times, and streaming down the aisle came four more ushers, all mean looking, all female, all in white blouses, average age sixty.

"Oh, all right," Calvin said in frustration, and rose to leave without battle.

"Calvin?" Mercredi whispered.

"What?" Calvin asked, a little annoyed.

"Slip me the camera."

"I'll take the camera, "Helga said with authority. And she did, snapping it out of Calvin's hands as a SWAT team of ushers escorted him to the lobby. Oh, the shame.

***

The good news was the bar was just about to open for intermission. This was not a great consolation, but it was some.

"Were you in watching Ray?" the bartender inquired while pouring Calvin a beer.

"Just for a flash," Calvin replied.

"Great isn't he, old Ray?" the bartender said more than asked.

"Oh, he sure is," Ray replied, somewhat disconsolate, as he took two drinks and then turned to look for a corner to stand in.

Mercredi was one of the first out at intermission and quickly found Calvin.

"Are you okay?" she asked.

"Oh ya, They roughed me up a little but I'm all right."

"Seriously, are you all right? I am so sorry."

"I'm fine," Calvin insisted, adding, "Here, I got you a glass of wine."

"You are so sweet, thank you."

"No problem. Shall we have these and then go?" Calvin asked.

"What, and miss the second half?" Mercredi asked with surprise.

"Well, it's just I can't see the second half, so..."

"Won't you wait for me?" she asked, with puppy dog eyes.

"Well, I guess." He did not sound too sure.

"Look at these great pictures I got after you left, Calvin," Mercredi said, beaming, and thrusting her cell phone in his face.

"I didn't leave, I was kicked out. And after all that you kept on taking pictures?"

"Of course, everyone was."

"Oh, I keep forgetting, everyone's doing it," Calvin said, with more than an ounce of sarcasm.

"Hey, do you still have your ticket?" Mercredi asked.

"Yes," Calvin replied, curiously.

Mercredi's face was the picture of pure optimism as she suggested, "Maybe you can come back in. We'll just go back in with the crowd; they won't notice you."

"Are you kidding?" Calvin demanded to know. "They even took my picture. They're probably printing up posters to put in the bathrooms right now."

"Oh come on; everyone's going in now, it can't hurt to try," she insisted.

"Oh, all right." Calvin felt he had said this before, a time or two, this evening. The crowd bottlenecked through the two entrances, east and west, to the theatre. Calvin and Mercredi went through the entrance farthest from their seats, reasoning it was less likely Helga would be there.

"And where do you think you're going?"

Calvin and Mercredi were wrong.

"Um, I just thought that, uh – "

"You thought wrong, Bub. Back you go." And back he did.

The good news was Mr. Charles' concert was visible on a closed-circuit TV mounted in the lobby. Calvin even managed to befriend the bartender who turned the volume up and together they sat, and watched, and drank. He was the bartender after all. Calvin reasoned that with all that had gone on, Mercredi could drive. So it was just like watching at home. Except you do not generally want it to be like that when you attend, in person, a live concert by one of music's greats.

***

The drive home was fairly quiet. It was not at first, what with Calvin drunkenly singing Christmas carols, but he soon fell asleep and that was over. In fact, Calvin did not even wake up as they went through the Starbucks drive-thru. Or the McDonald's drive-thru. Mercredi had to forcibly wake Calvin as she pulled the car into her driveway.

"Calvin, Calvin! Wake up!" she hollered anxiously as she started to shake him by the shoulder. "There's something wrong."

"I don't have your camera," Calvin responded in a daze.

"There's someone lying in the street," Mercredi explained in a concerned tone.

"What?" asked Calvin, as if hit by a shot of adrenaline. They both jumped out of the car and ran to the edge of the street. A figure in a hooded winter parka was lying face down until Mercredi and Calvin rolled it over. It was Helga.

"Oh my god," gasped Mercredi.

"She's unconscious. Do you have your cell phone?"

Alertly Mercredi handed her phone to Calvin. "It's on speed dial," she said.

"What is?"

"911."

"I've already dialed it. Hello? Yes we need an ambulance, at –"

Mercredi chimed in with, "522 Oceanview Road, Nanaimo."

Calvin repeated, "522 Oceanview Road, Nanaimo. A woman; it may have been a heart attack. I think she is. In her sixties for sure. Please hurry, we'll wait here."

As some of you know, and hopefully most of you do not, waiting ten minutes for an ambulance feels an eternity. Mercredi unwittingly broke the tension of the wait when she spoke. "Check her pockets."

"What?" Calvin asked, shocked.

"She may still have my camera. In one of her pockets. Check."

"I certainly am not checking an unconscious woman's pockets for your camera and neither are you," Calvin declared in no uncertain terms.

Before Mercredi could finish saying, "Pleeease," the unmistakeable sounds of sirens could be heard, and the next thing you knew Helga, pockets un-scavenged, was on a stretcher and being placed inside the ambulance. One of the ambulance attendants looked at Calvin,

"You coming?" Somewhat dumbfounded, Calvin said,

"Who, me?"

"Hurry up, get in," the attendant ordered while beginning to close the ambulance doors. Calvin did as he was told, and the next thing he knew he was in the back of a speeding ambulance, sirens blaring, racing down the highway to Nanaimo General Hospital.

"You the son?" the attendant asked as he sat down next to Calvin.

"Um, no, I don't really know her."

"You don't?"

"No, I found her."

"Well, she's lucky you did," the attendant offered. "Because of you she still has a chance."

"Only a chance?" Calvin asked.

"A chance is a good thing," the attendant explained. "I bet this isn't how you pictured spending Christmas Eve."

"No, I can't say it is," Calvin conceded. "What are you doing with that?" Calvin asked of the attendant, who had just taken a camera out of a drawer.

"I'm going to take her picture; I take every patient's picture," he answered.

"I wouldn't do that if I were you," Calvin said in earnest.

"Why not?" the attendant asked in a surprised voice.

"She's not a big fan of cameras," came the reply.

"I thought you didn't know her?"

"Well, I don't, but she was an usher at the Ray Charles concert tonight – "

"You went to Ray?" the attendant asked, interrupting, "How was he?"

"He was fine, the little I saw."

"You didn't see the whole show?" the attendant asked incredulously.

"No, I got kicked out, she..." Calvin said pointing down at Helga, "...kicked me out. For having a camera in the theatre."

"Well," the attendant said condescendingly, "You're not supposed to have a camera in a theatre, everyone knows that."

"Not everyone, believe me," Calvin replied with a sigh.

At that moment Helga began to convulse. "She's going into cardiac arrest," the attendant shouted. "Here take this," he said as he tossed the camera to Calvin. "Chuck, we're losing her," the attendant yelled toward the driver up front.

"Hang on, we're almost there," the driver yelled back. "Goddammed speed bumps!" And at that moment that is what the ambulance hit, a speed bump, at full speed. The ambulance leapt into the air. It came down with a bang and the camera rose out of Calvin's hands. Desperately his hands swung into the air trying to retrieve it, and as he caught it like an awkward wide receiver the unthinkable happened. The flash went off. Directly into the rear view mirror, temporarily blinding the driver. The loss of vision caused him to swerve and the ambulance hit the curb. Again it leapt into the air and Helga did too. Seemingly feet into the air, she came down with a thud as the emergency vehicle lurched to a sudden stop. A moment of silence, followed by the sputtering... of Helga. There on her chest lay, of all things, the curved end of a red-and-white candy cane. It seems the second jolt of the ambulance dislodged the candy, and now Helga continued to cough as she took in as much air as she could. She finally composed her breathing, and opened her eyes. There, above her, a concerned but relieved look on his face, was Calvin. Holding a camera.

"You!" Helga bellowed. Calvin was never so happy to be yelled at. Even by Helga. Especially by Helga.

"You!" he said with a laugh. "You're all right!"

"Of course I'm all right. Never been better in my life. 'Til I laid my eyes on you. How many cameras do you have?"

"Oh, this isn't mine," Calvin explained with a laugh.

"That's what you always say, isn't it sonny?"

"No, it really isn't. It's his."

"Stop trying to blame others and give me the camera," she ordered.

Helga grabbed the camera from Calvin, prompting the ambulance attendant to object, "Hey, give that to me, that's my camera." While removing said camera from Helga's paws the attendant continued, "And, you owe this man your life. He found you in the street, he called the ambulance, he even cleared your air passage way, 'though somewhat by accident."

"No, I meant to do that," Calvin added with a smirk.

"I'm in an ambulance?" Helga asked, softening somewhat.

The attendant confirmed, "You are in ambulance 1225, having arrived safely – for the most part – at Nanaimo General Hospital."

"For the most part," Calvin chipped in; "We're actually in a flower bed at the Nanaimo General Hospital, but close enough."

"So do you have anything to say now you know all this?" the attendant demanded of Helga.

"Yes," Helga replied. "I better have a private room!"

***

Soft, instrumental, Christmas music played in the hallway as Calvin and Mercredi, one carrying flowers and a plate of Nanaimo bars, and the other a wrapped Christmas present, made their way to the nurses' station.

"We're here to see Helga Bauer" Mercredi told the nurse on duty.

"You are?" the nurse asked, a little surprised. "No one's been in to see her all day, and it's Christmas."

"That's so sad," Mercredi said as she turned to Calvin.

"And you've brought a present. You must be family," the nurse remarked.

"Actually, the present is for you nurses. It's the kind of present you can drink, and it makes you feel better," Calvin explained.

Mercredi continued, "We sort of guessed you might have had a hard time with her today."

"NURSE!" The sound was unmistakable.

"All the way down the hall, as far as humanly possible, last door on the right," the nurse said, pointing one way and looking the other. "And tell Ms. Bauer I will be in to see her... right after my break."

Another burst of "NURSE!" greeted them like wind in a tunnel as Mercredi and Calvin opened the door to Helga's room.

Mercredi looked shocked. "Why all the wires?" she asked Calvin.

"They're monitoring her heart."

"I thought it was just something caught in her throat?"

"It was originally," Calvin said, "But the lack of oxygen that resulted led to other complications. They're just being cautious."

Mercredi looked up at Calvin, "Wouldn't lack of oxygen affect the brain?"

"Not hers," Calvin said plainly. "Not hers."

"Shall we go in?"

"Yes," Calvin replied, "But may I point out to you, this clearly written sign that says 'No electronic devices'. That would include cameras and cell phones. Okay?"

"Okay," Mercredi replied, trying to be good.

"It's you!" Helga bellowed as the two entered the room. Calvin braced himself for what might follow.

"Are you ever a sight for sore eyes," Helga declared in a complete change of tune. "You should see what I have had to put up with, with these nitwits in here. I swear they got their nurse's certificates on that web thingy."

Somewhat relieved at their greeting, notwithstanding the overall content, Calvin and Mercredi smiled and approached Helga's bed, a little bit braver now.

"These are for you," Mercredi informed her, extending her arm and offering the flowers to Helga.

"Poinsettias?" Helga asked. She seemed disappointed.

"And Nanaimo Bars," Calvin added. "That I made."

"Do you not like poinsettias?" Mercredi asked, sadly.

"I made the Nanaimo Bars," Calvin repeated.

Helga looked at the flowers a moment. "I love poinsettias," she said. "I can't think the last time someone gave me flowers. You two have made my Christmas a Christmas to remember. I know I am just a grumpy old woman, but I have this funny feeling that you have come into my life for a reason, and that you're going to change it somehow."

At that moment Mercredi's cell phone began to ring. "I'm sorry, I have to take this," Mercredi informed them while taking the device from her pocket.

"Nooooooo!" Calvin screamed, while diving toward her.

The End

Recipe for World Famous Nanaimo Bars

First Layer:

½ cup butter
¼ cup sugar
5 tbsp. cocoa
1 egg beaten
1 ¼ cups graham wafer crumbs
½ cup finely chopped pecans
1 cup coconut

Melt first 3 ingredients in top of double boiler. Add egg and stir to cook and thicken. Remove from heat. Stir in crumbs, coconut, and nuts. Press firmly into an ungreased 8" x 8" pan.

Second Layer:

½ cup butter
2 Tbsp. and 2 Tsp. cream
2 Tbsp. vanilla custard powder (Such as Bird's)
2 cups icing sugar

Cream butter, cream, custard powder, and icing sugar together well. Beat until light. Spread over bottom layer.

Third Layer:

4 squares semi-sweet chocolate (1 oz. each)
2 Tbsp. unsalted butter
Melt chocolate and butter over low heat. Cool. Once cool, but still liquid, pour over second layer and chill in refrigerator.

Chapter Four

THE CHRISTMAS MIRACLE   *by Hendrik Witmans*

Mary-Ann Coupar patiently waited her turn in the line-up at the Portal station. It was the day before Christmas, and she had just finished her London vacation. The shopping in Oxford street, the crowds in Soho, even late at night, it had all been fantastic. But now it was time to go home to celebrate Christmas with the Goodbine family. Her uncle, Bill Goodbine, was CEO of the company that made teleportation possible, and the whole family was gathering for Christmas at his mansion on a large acreage on Bowen Island, near Vancouver.

Mary-Ann was twenty-six and had been born before the dawn of teleportation. She knew about the excitement and the frustrations that went with organizing a long trip the old way. Flights had to be booked, there were cab rides to the airports, the line-ups, the waiting, the security problems, and the gruelling eight or nine hours in a claustrophobic plane cabin. People had to make arrangements for their vacation months ahead. All that had changed with teleportation. True, there was still a bit of paperwork, and on special times like Christmas, the portals could be busy. But compared to the old way, today's traveling was effortless.

The line was moving fast, as the station had two Portals. She pushed her suitcase on wheels ahead of her, clutching her handbag to her chest. It was almost unimaginable that within five minutes or less, she'd step out of the Portal in Vancouver, more than five thousands miles away. Mary-Ann had been orphaned at age four, when her parents died during a fire in an East Vancouver apartment. The last thing her Dad had done before he died, was throw his daughter out of the window on the sixth floor, onto a large bed-spread that neighbours had held up to break her fall. Aunt Evelyn and Uncle Bill had looked after her from that day on.

"Can I see your reservation pass, please?" The handsome young man at the counter smiled at her, waiting. She quickly handed him her papers, and he began to type her name into a keyboard to clear her with Immigration. It didn't take long: Coupar was Evelyn's maiden name, and it was almost as famous as the name Goodbine. Within minutes she was ushered into the Portal and stepped onto the small round platform from where she would be teleported. Her suitcase stood on a second platform.

"Stand still, please." The Portal attendant was an older lady, who had obviously done this thing many times. Her hands flew over a keyboard, and then she looked up and smiled at Mary-Ann. "Have a good trip, Miss Coupar."

Mary-Ann closed her eyes firmly, so she wouldn't see what would happen to her body. She always did in teleportation. Even after having been teleported more than twenty times, Mary-Ann still felt squeamish about the whole thing. She really wasn't very interested in technology, and she just couldn't understand how it was possible to take a human body apart into zillions of pieces, broadcast them all across the world, like radio waves, and then put them all back together again. Yet somehow it worked. Good thing it only lasted a few seconds. She heard the familiar hum of the scanner, then felt the curious light-headedness that always accompanied teleportation. The next thing she would see was Uncle Bill's smiling face.

Only it didn't quite turn out like that. When she opened her eyes, it was immediately obvious that things were wrong. Deadly wrong! She was not standing on a Portal platform, nor was anyone there to meet her. She wasn't even in a building, but in a forest, among thousands of trees, and ferns. And it wasn't cool, like Vancouver in December, but hot, stifling, tropically hot. And it was noisy: she could hear birds, crickets, monkeys, and other unknown creatures. Fear tightened her chest. Where in heaven's name was she?

She looked at her body to make sure she was in one piece. Before she started to search for her suitcase, she knew it wouldn't be there. Wherever she was, all she had with her, were her clothes and her handbag. She quickly opened her bag and took out her cell phone, hoping against hope. There was no signal. And there was absolutely no sign of a Portal station. She closed her eyes again, like an ostrich that stuck its head in the sand, hoping that the threat would go away. Of course it didn't, and reality began to sink in on Mary-Ann: she was alone, stranded without any resources, food or drinks, in a tropical forest, goodness knew how far from civilization. She was already boiling hot, and would need water pretty soon. Panic gripped her by the throat, and she could hardly swallow. She was going to die!

Apart from the early tragedy, things had always been easy for Mary-Ann. Being related to Bill Goodbine, the multi-billionaire, had been her ticket to a comfortable, "not a care in the world" lifestyle. She had gone to college to get her Bachelor degree, then kept on studying Sociology for a Masters degree, and she was working on her PhD. She had never needed to work, had never wanted for anything, and was totally unprepared for a situation like this. But she knew she needed to act, and soon, or she would die of heat exhaustion. She swung her bag over her shoulder and began to explore her new, hostile environment.

It was hard going. There was no sign of a path, or a clearing; just dense, tropical foliage all around. She tried to make room by grabbing ferns and leaves and pulling them out, but the sharp edges only cut her hands. She found a stick and began to slash it around, using it like a machete. It was useless

"HELP! Is anyone there? I need help, please!" She called out as loud as she could, but the only response was a scurrying of something in the bush behind her, probably a monkey, or a bird. Why should there be anyone around in the first place? Her dress clang onto to her like a wet towel, and she knew she couldn't go on much longer. Was this how it was going to end? Would she die here, not even knowing where she was? She suddenly realized what an empty life she'd led, despite all the family's money. She had very few real friends, no boyfriend, and now she was going to die at age twenty-six, because something had gone horribly wrong during that stupid teleporting process. After struggling for a few more minutes she had made a small clearing and she collapsed, knowing she would never get up again.

* * *

It was cooler, and less noisy. When Mary-Ann came to, she noticed she was no longer in the forest. She lay on a mattress in some kind of room, and it was much darker. She had no idea how she got where she was and she felt quite groggy. On further inspection, the room appeared to be a wooden lean-to, suspended on one end by a large tree branch and on the other by two wooden sticks in the ground. She could hear water running, somewhere. Water! She sat up, suddenly remembering everything. Then all her alarms kicked in. Something, or someone was coming!

A man loomed in front of the lean-to. He was carrying a pail of water, and looked quite old, at least seventy, Mary-Ann guessed. He was dressed in the most horrible rags she had ever seen: a half-torn dirty khaki shirt, ragged-edged shorts that revealed thin, varicose legs, no socks, and the remnants of what once had been Adidas sneakers. The man's hair and beard hadn't seen a barber or scissors for a long time. While he stood there, he suddenly gave her a wide smile, and she noticed he had only three teeth left.

"American? Si? Aqua?" He put the pail beside her, and Mary-Ann cupped her hand, and scooped the cool liquid up and brought it to her mouth. It was the best water she had ever tasted. She drank noisily while the other watched her, smiling. When she had had enough, Mary-Ann took one last scoop and splashed it all over her face. Then she turned to the man.

"Thank you, for the water and for saving my life. I'm Canadian. You speak English? Where is this place?"

"Is El Salvador. I speak little English."

"What is your name?"

"Jorge Fernandez."

"I am Mary-Ann Coupar. Look, Jorge, I can't possibly explain. You know about teleportation?"

He just looked at her, shaking his head.

"Never mind, I really must make a phone call. Where is the nearest telephone?"

"Ah, el telefono. No. Not here."

"All right, where is the nearest city?

"Many hours driving. But no car. Is San Salvador."

Brilliant. Stranded in the jungle with an old man who hardly spoke English. The day before Christmas. Mary-Ann didn't know whether to laugh or cry. But at least she had water, and if Jorge lived here, there had to be food around also.

"What about a village? A place with a few shops?"

"Ah, tienda, yes, shops. No, not here. Tomorrow, barge. On water. River, not far. Bring goods. You rest. Talk later. Use more water. I go now." Jorge turned round, and hobbled away in his worn sneakers.

It was quite pleasant in the coolness of the approaching evening. She wondered how long she had been out, when Jorge had found her. She sat up, and looked at the pail with water, a precious commodity here, no doubt. She quickly took another sip and splashed some on her hands and neck. Then she sat up.

Time to take stock. She opened her handbag and took everything out, putting in on the mattress next to her. A nail clipper. A compact. Yeah, that would really come in handy here! A note book and pen. A bottle of Tylenol. A roll of peppermint. A map of London. Her useless cell phone. A small box of Kleenex. And a Tampax tampon. She almost laughed out loud. The last thing she took out was her wallet. Four credit cards, a Canadian driver's license, a bunch of loose change, and two hundred dollars. That was all she had, and the clothes she was wearing.

Jorge was back. He was carrying a little bag and he walked over to a cardboard box, that apparently held his belongings. He took an old rusty knife from the box and handed it to her with a papaya.

"You eat," he said. Mary-Ann had to admit she was ravenous, and she quickly began to peel the fruit, and soon she was enjoying it, the juice running all around her mouth. Jorge sat down next to her. He seemed to be quite nimble for his age.

"You travel, for Christmas, yes?" he asked.

She nodded. "I'm supposed to be in Vancouver, with my family, but something went wrong. Have you got family, Jorge?"

"Si. A son, and wife, not here. We not speak." It was almost as if a cloud passed over his happy face.

"If you don't mind me asking, Jorge, aren't you a bit old to live here, in the middle of nowhere, all by yourself? It must be very difficult. "

He paused for a second, as if his mind needed the time to translate. "Si, I am seventy-two years, but I am criminal. I kill person. Important person. I wanted by policia."

"How long have you been here?"

"Twenty-five years."

She looked at him. While she had lived a life of luxury out in Canada, this poor man had lived under a lean-to, without anything. He had committed a crime, that was true, but still it seemed awful. She waited, not wanting to intrude in his personal life.

"I was policia," he said, after a while. "My wife . . . she eh, adulterio?"

"See was unfaithful to you?"

"Si. There was other man. I found, and shot him. Dead. He was also policia. My comandante. After that, I am wanted man."

"And your wife?"

"She left."

"I see. And your son was in the police force also?"

The old man nodded. "He is, how do you say, lista negra."

"I don't know what that means. Was he involved in the shooting?"

"No, no. Him, no more promotion."

"I see. He was blacklisted for what you did, and now you don't talk. That's sad."

"Si."

For a while they sat in silence listening to the cacophony of creatures in the jungle. It was almost dark, and with the dark came the mosquitoes. Mary-Ann suddenly felt depressed. She couldn't imagine living here for twenty five days, let alone twenty-five years. She had to get to a city to find a Portal, or at least a phone. But how?

Jorge stirred and stood up. "You sleep here," he said, pointing at the mattress. "I keep watch."

"Are you expecting trouble?"

"No trouble. Sometimes animals. Monkeys, maybe wild dogs. I have gun." He walked over to his box with personal belongings and came back with some kind of netting.

"For mosquito's," he said, smiling. "Buenos noches." He picked up a small handgun from his box and walked to a small tree trunk, away from the lean-to, and lay down, resting his back against it.

For Mary-Ann sleep was out of the question. Tomorrow was Christmas, and she was thousands of miles away from her family, who by now probably thought she was dead. She felt utterly dirty and hot, and the netting didn't do a good job. She was assaulted by mosquitoes. Suddenly she cried softly, lying on a filthy old mattress that she would have thrown into the garbage at home! She had no pillows, and her head was only supported by a fold in the mattress. After a while she calmed down. At least she wasn't alone. She felt comfortable with Jorge, despite what he had done in his life. If he wanted to harm her he could have done so already. Perhaps tomorrow they could go to that barge, and find help. For a while she listened to the never-ending hum and droning of the forest, and eventually nature took its course and she fell asleep.

* * *

She woke up with the sun in her face, and the noise of sizzling in her ears. Jorge was standing in the little clearing next to the lean-to, and he had made a fire. On an improvised stove, made of an iron grid resting on two rocks, stood a saucepan with four eggs, being fried. Eggs?

"Good morning," she said. "Where on earth did you find eggs?"

"Chickens, in forest. I find. We eat now, yes?"

"O.K. But afterwards I have to find that place where you get water. I have to wash. Can we go to that barge, please?"

"Si. Barge arrives noon, maybe. Two hours walk. Leave soon."

"Right."

The eggs were absolutely delicious, and this time there was a mango. Jorge had also got fresh water for her. After breakfast, Mary-Ann stood up. "Do you have soap?"

"Qué?"

"Soap, you know? For washing?" She pretended to wash her face.

"Ah! Jabón." He shook his head. "No. You get on barge."

"Can you please show me where the water is?"

Jorge led her to a small stream nearby, and she was disappointed. She could freshen up, but there was no place to swim.

"Find way back?" Jorge asked, politely. He obviously wanted to give her privacy.

"Yes, thank you. I won't be long." First things first. After Jorge had left, she squatted near the river and relieved herself. Then she stripped off her dirty clothes and washed herself as best as she could. Too bad there was no time to wash her clothes. When she felt reasonably clean, she dressed again and headed back to the lean-to. The temperature was very pleasant, but that would probably change soon.

Jorge was waiting for her, carrying a small bag, and a long machete.

"We go?"

"I'm ready."

It was a thousand times easier than when she had been alone. Obviously, Jorge went to the river regularly, and had cleared a path before. He was using his machete only occasionally. But the going was still tough, and the temperature was keeping up with the time: the later it got, the warmer. If only she had a change of clothes! She must stink a mile way. The scenery changed a bit, the forest was less dense and there were open spaces with grass, and for a while it got hillier. After about an hour, she simply couldn't go on any further, and she motioned Jorge to stop.

"I need to rest, please, Jorge. Just for a few minutes."

It took about twenty minutes for her to get going again, and Mary-Ann hoped they wouldn't miss the barge. Jorge seemed to have an inexhaustible supply of energy, despite his age. When they came closer to the river it became easier, and finally, Jorge stood on top of a small hill, and pointed below.

"Lempa." The view was beautiful, as the river Lempa flowed down below, its water silvery in the sun. There was a landing of some kind, and a vessel was tied up.

"That's the barge?"

"Si. We lucky. It come on time."

The barge was the closest thing to civilization that Mary-Ann had seen in two days. It was like an open market, with scores of people meandering around tables set up on deck. When they approached the barge it became apparent that Jorge, like most men, didn't really like shopping.

"You look," he said. "I get few things, then meet here. Si?"

"All right." Mary-Ann rushed to the stands. She was the only white woman, and she could see the looks of surprise on most of the other women's faces. Like any market, people were talking and shouting, but it was all in Spanish and she didn't understand a word of it. She walked to the first table she got to and spoke to the woman behind it.

"Excuse me, I am from Canada. do you speak English?"

The woman smiled at her. "Canadiense, bueno. You here holiday?"

"No. Do you have a phone?" she asked, but the woman didn't understand.

"El telephono?"

The merchant shook her head, and pointed a bony hand high up at the coastline, and rattled off something in Spanish. Mary-Ann didn't understand a word of it. She walked off and addressed another woman at the next stall, but she ignored her. Another man, standing behind a table with magazines and books, didn't have a clue what she said, and just stared at her as if she was an apparition. Damn, how difficult could it be to find a telephone! This was 2025, for Pete's sake! Mary-Ann was getting quite irate. She saw an official looking older man, perhaps the supervisor, or owner of the barge. The barge had to go somewhere afterwards, a village or a small town. The goods came from somewhere. Perhaps she could buy herself a passage. She was about to walk over to the man and ask him when something began to stir inside her, as she remembered what day it was.

It was Christmas Day! A time to enjoy with friends, to relax and share good food, give presents. Fate had given her an opportunity to celebrate a unique Christmas this year, and all she did was think of herself and run away from it! What about Jorge? He was so nice to her, and he had saved her life. Shouldn't she do something in return? The least she could do was cook him a nice Christmas dinner! The thought made her suddenly feel much better, and she began to wander around the tables like a tourist, looking for bargains.

The market turned out to be a bit of a disappointment. There were all kinds of fresh fruit and vegetables, but the other stuff looked as if it belonged in a flea market or garage sale. It was a mishmash of items: old lamps, motors, knives, old radios and televisions, She very much doubted if anything was new. There was also a stand selling life stock: chickens, baby pigs, monkeys. Mary-Ann noticed a stand that sold soap and she quickly bought two bars, paying with a twenty dollar bill. The young man behind the table didn't blink an eyelid, wrapped up the bars, and handed her a handful of coins. She had no idea how much it was.

The food table was a disaster. Most of the meat and cheeses looked well past their best-by date. and there were flies all over the place. She had no idea what kind of meat it was. Could be monkey, or dog, for all she knew. She finally decided to play it safe and settled on a large tin of corned beef. From a fruit stand she bought a large sweet potato, two bananas, some mushrooms. and something that looked like eggplant. To her surprise, she noticed a six-pack of Heineken among the fruit and she bought that also. Might as well have a real party! She awkwardly put everything in the two bags the man behind the table supplied, and after paying him, she decided it would be enough. Time to go back. Then she noticed the sneakers.

They were thrown on a large table, full of clothing of various kinds: colorful tee shirts, sweaters, trousers, all mixed up in a large pile. The sneakers were Nike and they looked fairly new. She picked them up, wondering if they were Jorge's size. They looked about right. She thought about going back and ask him to try them on, but that would ruin the surprise. She noticed a duffle-bag and picked it up also. Perfect. She rummaged some more through the clothes, and found a nice shirt, a pair of shorts, and socks also. To her delight, she found a colorful dress that might just fit her. She turned to the man behind the stand. He had dark brown skin, and black hair, like everyone else. He had seen her pick up the items, and eyed her suspiciously

"Do you speak English?"

He shook his head. "Triste."

She pointed at the duffle-bag, the shoes, shirt, socks, shorts, and the dress.

"How much for all these, in dollars?"

"Ciento veinte."

She held out a bundle of dollars, and was shocked when he pointed at a hundred dollar bill and a twenty! It would leave her with exactly sixty dollars, and a pocketful of useless coins! How could she get to San Salvador on that?

There were some other customers waiting, and the man was staring at her, as if to prompt her to make a decision. "All right," she said, remembering it was Christmas. She paid the merchant and put everything in the duffle-bag, the shoes first. It was very heavy, and she wondered how she was ever going to carry it all the way back. Nodding goodbye to the merchant, she slung the bag over her shoulder and headed back to meet Jorge. While she walked past the river, she noticed it was quite murky, with patches of oil, probably from the barge. She would have liked to go for a swim, but not here, and certainly not without a swimsuit in front of the people. When the old man saw her coming, his eyebrows shot up in surprise.

"You buy so much? Here, I carry."

The way back was just as hard, and when they finally reached the lean-to it was late afternoon. Mary-Ann put the duffle-bag on the floor and flopped on the mattress, exhausted. After a few minutes, she opened the bag and rummaged to find the beers. She took two out and handed one to Jorge. The old man gratefully accepted. Luckily he had an opener on an old rusty Swiss army knife. They sat down, enjoying the warm beer. When she had finished, Mary-Ann turned to Jorge.

"I'm making us a Christmas dinner," she said. "Can you make a fire, please, while I go and wash?"

"Si." He busied himself with twigs and branches while Mary-Ann took her new dress and the soap out of the duffle-bag and headed towards the stream. She quickly stripped off and washed herself as best as she could, this time with soap. It was lovely, but she should have bought a towel. She waited for awhile, to let herself dry in the sun. Then she put on her new dress. It wasn't a bad fit. It had colorful flowers all over it: daisies and buttercups. The dress was a bit large, and billowy, but that would be lovely in the heat. She put her dirty clothes in the water and rubbed them together with soap, then rinsed everything out. When she had finished, she headed back and presented herself to Jorge.

"Well, what do you think?" She pirouetted in front of him. The old man smiled at her.

"You. Filmstar? Si? Beautiful!"

Mary-Ann suddenly felt embarrassed and she quickly walked away to hang her wet dress on a branch to dry. Then she began to prepare their dinner. There was a slight problem: Jorge had cutlery, but no plates, and only one saucepan. It was still dirty from that morning. Time to improvise. She took the saucepan, and the water pail and walked back to the creek again. She washed the saucepan, filled the pail, and headed back.

"Jorge, have you got something flat that I can work on? A board?" She gestured with her hands.

The old man stood thinking for a while, then his face lit up. "Si." He walked around to the back of the lean-to and came back carrying a square sheet of metal. It advertised Corona, the Mexican beer. "More," he said, and walked off into the woods. When he returned, he carried two logs and put them down on the ground, then put the sheet over it.

"Perfect," Mary-Ann got one of the knives and began to prepare the mushrooms, sweet potato and the eggplant. She cut everything up and put it all in the saucepan. She added some water, then, carefully balancing the saucepan, she walked over to the fire that Jorge had started. She put the pan on top of the grate, then frowned. What about plates?

"We need something to eat from, Jorge. Have you got anything?" He stood for a minute, and scratched his head. Then he held up his hand, picked up his machete and disappeared in the jungle. She heard him hack about for a few seconds, than he was back with two large ferns, and Mary-Ann laughed out loud. Talk about improvising! Still, it might work. She took the ferns and laid them flat on their makeshift table. Then the waiting was for the vegetables.

"So what do we do tomorrow?" she asked, sitting down on her mattress. "Will that barge still be there?"

"No, leaves tonight. Back next week."

"Can you get me to San Salvador somehow?"

"We try. But difficult. First walk to friend, two hours. He has car. Then four hours drive. He take you, not me. Danger. Bad people on roads, sometimes."

"Does your friend have a phone?"

Jorge nodded. "But not working. Two days ago, big trouble on mountain. How you say, terremoto. The earth. It moves."

"An earth quake?"

"Si. No phone."

So the phone lines were down. Brilliant. When the vegetables were done, Mary-Ann carefully took the pan, drained it to the side of the fire, and placed it on their table. She opened the can of corned beef, halved it. and put the halves on their improvised plates, then added the vegetables. Some of the juices ran off the ferns, but they served their purpose.

"There. Our Christmas dinner, Jorge. It was the best I could do." She could see the old man was impressed.

"You, good cook!"

The long trip had made her hungry, and Jorge also, it seemed. It was actually quite good, and for a while they sat in quiet, eating. She wondered what the family on Bowen Island would think about her Christmas dinner. What a laugh! They'd be eating a three course dinner: pheasant, or turkey, with all the trimmings, and chocolate cake, or Christmas pudding for dessert! She really had to contact them soon, they must be awfully worried about her. For the first time, she wondered what could have gone wrong. How could she have materialized without a Portal station?

After the meal, they sat back and relaxed. Then Mary-Ann pulled the dufflebag closer.

"Jorge, in Canada, we have a habit of giving presents on Christmas Day. So I bought something for you." She grabbed in the bag, and took out the shirt she had bought, and handed it to Jorge. He was astonished.

"For me?"

"Of course. No one else here."

It was a disaster. Jorge took off his old rags, but when he put the new shirt on, Mary-Ann's spirits plummeted. The shirt was too small, and Jorge couldn't even do the buttons up.

"Gracias! I wear, like this." He turned around and she saw his hairy chest between the two sides of the shirt. If Jorge had been forty years younger it would have been quite sexy. Next the shorts. Mary-Ann demurely turned around, while Jorge took off his old shorts, and put the new ones on. They more or less fitted, and it was a marked improvement. Jorge stood up and was about to walk away.

"No wait, there is more."

"More?"

She handed him the socks. He sat down and with some difficulty took off the remains of his runners. His feet looked absolutely atrocious, and Mary-Ann figured that a podiatrist would either run away in horror, or wring his hands in glee at the prospect of so many hours of work. Jorge hadn't clipped his toenails for most of his life, it seemed. The nails were all sharp and much too big. They would ruin the new socks!

"Jorge, wait. I have nail clippers, and I'll cut your toenails for you. Sit down on that log over there." She pointed at the log that Jorgen had slept against the night before. He obediently walked over and sat down, while Mary-Ann squatted in front of him and began to cut his toenails. It was quite a job, like mowing the grass with a pair of scissors. But she persisted, and after a while Jorge's feet looked more presentable.

"There! Now you can put on your socks."

The socks fitted well, and Jorge reached for his old shoes, but Mary-Ann held his arm.

"No wait. This is your last present, Jorge." She handed him the sneakers. "Thank you for all you did for me. Merry Christmas."

Time seemed to stand still. Jorge stared at his new shoes, as if they were made of gold. He carefully turned them over and studied the rubber pattern on the soles. Then he delicately pulled back the laces, pulling each lace separately. He put the right shoe down and began to put his foot inside. Mary-Ann could hear a drum roll in her head, and her heart was pounding. "Please, Lord, let them be the right size!"

Jorge's foot went in without any trouble. The left shoe was next. It also fitted perfectly. The old man stood up to his full height, and beamed, like a young child that got its first toy.

"Gracias! Thank you!" He reached over, grabbed Mary-Ann by the shoulders, and pulled her close. Then he planted a big kiss on her cheek.

"I wear. Every day."

Mary-Ann felt as if a weight was lifted off her chest. It had all worked out. Christmas had been a success, whatever happened next. She began to clear their improvised table, while Jorge walked around trying out his new shoes When she had finished, it had gone almost dark, and they sat down outside the lean-to, listening to the cacophony in the trees and looking at the stars. She had never seen such a beautiful sky. There was no moon, and without the lights of urbanisation the sky was just covered in a mosaic of sparkling specks, some bright, others in groups she could hardly see.

"So, Jorge, why don't you move to a village to be with other people? Why live your life here, all alone?"

"Dangerous. Spies, in many places. If found, I shot."

"What about other countries? Honduras? Belize? Mexico?"

"No passport. Cannot leave country."

For a while she thought of Jorge's dilemma. Surely, there was something else he could do? Or was he perhaps quite happy to be alone? She looked up at the sky again and saw one bright star, and it reminded her of the Star of Bethlehem.

"You know about stars, Jorge? What's that one called?"

Jorgen looked up for a moment and studied the firmament. Then he shook his head.

"No star. Too big."

She looked up again. It was true, the star had grown twice its size in a few seconds. Then she sat straight up and listened. What was that noise? Woosh, woosh. Very faintly, but louder by the second. She suddenly knew, and she jumped up, grabbing Jorge by the shoulders, and pulled him along, dancing around the clearing. "It's a helicopter! They have found me!"

They both stared at the sky, as the star indeed turned into a helicopter with a searchlight that began to light up the entire area. Mary-Ann started running around, waving her arms, shouting.

"It's me. I'm here!"

There was no place to land, and the helicopter kept hovering right above them. Then a door opened, and a man was lowered on a rope, and even before he reached the ground, Mary-Ann knew it was her Uncle. She rushed over to meet him.

Bill Goodbine reached the ground and hugged his niece, as if he hadn't seen her in twenty years. He was crying.

"Oh, my God, you're safe, Mary-Ann! You've no idea what we went through. Are you all right?"

"Yes, fine," she said, sniffing. "Thanks to Jorge, here. He saved my life."

Bill Goodbine turned around, walked over to Jorge, and shook his hand for the longest time.

"Bill Goodbine. Thanks for rescuing my niece, Jorge. We are greatly indebted to you."

"Si," Jorge smiled. "Your niece. She good cook!"

It broke the ice, and they all laughed. Mary-Ann pulled her uncle away. "Can't we take Jorge with us? He's lived here for twenty-five years, all by himself, poor man."

"Why? Is he hiding from something?"

"Yes. He's wanted by the police."

"Well, in that case, no. No way can we take him back to Canada. It'd open up the proverbial can of worms. Anyway, we must get going. We haven't asked for permission to fly in this airspace, and we don't want the whole El Salvador air force after us."

"Can't you at least give him some money?"

"Sure." Bill took out his wallet and they walked back to Jorge.

"There you are," Bill said, handing the old man a big wad of hundred dollar bills. "Thanks for everything."

The old man waved his hands in front of him.

"No, no! No money. I have presents." He pointed at his shirt, shorts and shoes. "Thank you, Mary-Ann!"

"O.K. you go first," Bill said.

"No, you go. I want to say goodbye to Jorge."

Bill pulled the rope and grabbed it tight. "Don't be long," he said, while he was winched up. Mary-Ann walked over to Jorge, and stood in front of him. She suddenly cried, and threw her arms around the old man, pulling him close. She tried to find a spot of skin on his cheek to kiss him, but gave up and just kissed his beard. Then she reached in her purse and took out a little bag, made of rumpled paper.

"Just coins, Jorge. I won't need them. And also, the nail clippers, for future use." She gave him a difficult smile. "Take care of yourself, Jorge, and God Bless."

The old man held her tight for a moment.

"Merry Christmas, Mary-Ann." Jorge also smiled, but his eyes were wet.

In the light from the searchlight, Mary Ann saw her dress hanging from the branch and she rushed over to get it. Then she noticed Jorge, bringing the duffelbag.

"No, you keep the bag, Jorge. It's more use to you than to me."

Then it was time to go. One last smile, then she pulled the rope and was slowly hoisted into the helicopter. Inside, it was pandemonium. Evelyn was there, and Tim, their son. Everyone hugged her for the longest time, and they all cried a bit. Then they strapped in, and Bill told the pilot to leave in a hurry.

"You've created quite a stir, you know, Mary-Ann," Bill said. "We call you the Christmas Miracle. We still don't know what went wrong. You were actually received in Vancouver, but then there was an explosion, and you were transmitted out again, but your assembly had already started, and somehow you ended up where you did. Nobody can explain it. We had a hell of a time finding you, but we finally managed to trace your Bio-signal into the general direction you had been sent. But we would never have found you without the GPS signal in your cell phone. It was a very weak, and we still weren't sure we had the right spot, until I saw you. You've given us all a whole new idea, you know. A whole new direction in teleportation. Perhaps it is possible to teleport people without terminals! We're working on it all ready. All thanks to you."

Mary-Ann looked down but she couldn't see anything. The jungle was just one dark mass below. She hadn't heard a word her uncle said. All she could think of was a lonely old man, living in a rickety lean-to, and the look on his face when she had presented him with a new pair of shoes.

Recipe for Impromptu Christmas Dinner

Ingredients:

1 can of Corned Beef
1 medium sweet potato
1 medium eggplant
1 can of beer
Mushrooms
Paprika, salt, pepper (if available)

Wash and dice the sweet potato. Do not peel!

Peel and dice the eggplant.

Put both in a medium frying pan, add the mushrooms, and half a can of beer. Let simmer on low heat for about fifteen minutes.

Cut and dice the corned beef. Add to the mixture.

Cover and let simmer for an additional five minutes, then add the other half of the beer, if you haven't drunk it at this stage!

Add spices, and you're done! Should serve two.

The above recipe is entirely a product of the writer's imagination. Any resemblance to real cooking is purely coincidental.

Enjoy!

Chapter Five

A FATHER'S LOVE   by Lorhainne Eckhart

December 24, 1926

"Make sure you and Rose are back before sundown."

Fourteen-year-old David Lattimer couldn't contain his excitement, no more than he could hold back a big toothy grin as he waved to his father outside their four-room log cabin. Smoke drifted neatly from the stovepipe into the chilly island air.

David trudged through the damp underbrush wearing three pairs of thick wool socks in his father's old, loose leather boots. Rose, his ten-year-old sister, dogged his heals as she did every day. Her pigtails stuck out from under the ridiculous wool green hat he'd swear had been a cast off from the poor box. Rose was a tiny sprite of a girl, with freckles and brown eyes, wearing his old brown coat over his too small overalls. On her, she had to roll up the pant legs and stuff the edges into her black boots, which did come from the poor box.

Rose skipped ahead of David, swinging her arms.

"Rose, stay behind me. The path's too narrow up here, and you're going to be soaked before I find the goose." He expected her to whine – complain—to argue. However, she surprised the heck out of him when she obediently pulled in behind him on the narrow path, in the thick forest filled with old fir and cedar on the 40-acre parcel owned by his family near Cameron Lake, on Vancouver Island.

David's longish hair drooped in front of his eyes. He yanked off his red woollen mitten with his teeth and tucked his thick brown hair under his dark wool cap. He knew it was time for a haircut when his mother teased he was beginning to look like a girl.

Over his left shoulder, David cradled the Winchester ten-gauge single load shotgun. The one bequeathed from Grandfather George. He took his role as big brother seriously, making sure the gun wasn't pointed at Rose.

David grinned; he still couldn't believe his Father's surprise this morning. This year, David got to hunt the Christmas Goose. A tradition passed down by his Grandfather, to his father. He patted his right pocket, to double check the ten spare shell casings were still where he'd put them.

"How far do we have to walk? And where are we going to find the goose?" Rose had such a high-pitched voice, at times chattering non-stop that his poor ears ached from listening to her rattle on. If he didn't answer her, she'd keep asking.

"We'll head down towards Cameron Lake. That's where Dad and I saw a school of winter geese the other day."

"But that's an hour away." Rose trailed behind, her voice squeaked like a wagon wheel that needed greasing. David was tempted to tell her to go home. But he wanted that goose, and knew his father would be angry if Rose went home alone.

"Would you stop complaining. You didn't have to come." David walked faster because he knew that'd really piss her off.

A tightly packed snowball slammed the back of his head, causing David to stumble. He spun around and glared at his stubborn little sister. What stung more, his head or pride, David wasn't sure. Short, tough, and determined, described Rose to a tee. Her lips scrunched up like a mad little bee. David knew first hand her fiery temper would lead her head on into a scrap. Why, just last week she sucker punched him with a solid jab to the bridge of his nose, and he'd swear he'd bled like a stuck pig. But then she'd caught him off guard, entirely by surprise, which was a low blow. Even his parents had been furious, but then they didn't know he'd goaded her. By laughing at the silly nickname, the boys had cat-called Rose at school over and over. "Sweepy." And that was all because Mama waved goodbye to Rose, calling her Sweet Pea in front of the town kids.

Nevertheless, his Daddy drilled into him some hard honourable lessons; no matter what you don't hit a girl, ever. And right now he wanted to shoot a goose, not scrap with Rose. So, David swallowed his pride and nearly choked on the hard lump burning his throat. What he did do was walk faster still. Let her run.

"David, slow down, you're going too fast. David, aren't you going to answer me?"

David whipped around so fast Rose bumped into him. "No, Rose! Stop it. I'm not going to fight with you. All I want is to find the geese, shoot one and go home. That's it, and if you're going to keep talking, you're gonna scare them away, so be quiet." He didn't wait for a response. David hurried through the brush staying on the same familiar trail that wound its way down to the lake. To Rose's credit, she didn't argue. She closed her mouth, let out a huff, and dogged David's heels again.

They strode lower into the valley. The air was damper, heavier with mist. He knew they were close to the lake. A thick mix of fir, cedar and alder trees surrounded them and formed an umbrella overhead. The overgrown path, which had most likely been created by antelope and deer, led down to their water source. David patted the twin fir. This was the lower part of the trail right before the open grove, not far from the lake.

A glimmer of black flashed from the corner of his eye. He sucked a breath, then another, before it registered in his head what that was. But by then his heart had already slammed his throat shut, choking off any reasonable sound while his back broke out in a cold, prickly sweat. "Get up a tree!" David somehow managed to croak out the panicked words, even to his own ears the low scratchy voice didn't sound anything like his.

David swivelled his head between a bundled up Rose who stood frozen as a mouse, and the curious bear cub. Her mouth gaped, and her big eyes filled with fear, a poison which squeezed the hair up the back of David's neck.

"Back away move slowly toward the tree, hurry Rose." She didn't move. David backed away from the cub and stepped on Rose's foot. Her breath wheezed, maybe that's what knocked some sense into her. She grabbed his arm with a shaky hand and moved.

A second cub wandered from behind the old cedar. Rose stumbled. "Get up Rose." And she did just as David somehow boosted her up, so she could grab the first branch. She'd just scampered onto the branch when a low growl split the icy air, and crashed through the underbrush. David didn't know how he did it, but somehow he leaped six feet up onto the first thick branch. Planting his hand on Rose's butt, he shoved hard. "Faster, go Rose go! She's right behind us!"

Reach, pull, step. One foot after the other, he climbed each thick branch of this Douglas Fir. Rose was quick and appeared to fly up the tree as she grabbed a branch pushed off grabbed the next, higher and higher until they climbed more than halfway up that old growth tree. And when David glanced down his blood turned to ice as he stared at the steel shotgun in the dirt, right where Mama bear circled in fury. She growled and pawed at the base of the tree, while her cubs wandered behind her.

"David, is it a Black Bear?"

"Yes dangit. And she's not happy."

Rose dangled on the branch above him. She was breathing heavily, as if she'd raced up a mountain. David held onto the branch above him and glanced up. Her large, innocent eyes pleaded for him to do something. They had to be about a hundred feet up, high enough to be safe unless Mama decided to come after them.

"What is a black bear and her cubs doing out this time of year? Aren't they supposed to be hibernating?"

The bear continued to charge, crazed, her wispy snarl short and rough, as she dug and clawed at the ground, circling the tree.

"David, is she going to climb up here? What are we going do?" Rose perched on the branch above him.

"I don't know." David was abrupt.

Rose began to whimper above him. David couldn't console her; he had enough to do holding himself together. Tears burned his eyes, and his throat throbbed with something thick and gooey. How long would it be before their father would come looking for them? He hoped it'd be soon; except his stomach sank with the realization that Dad wouldn't start looking until sundown. Then how far would he get in the dark? It was cold. Neither was prepared for this. How would they survive a night in this old fir tree?

All he could focus on was the twisting agony that shot like nails up his back, shoulders and legs, from sitting balanced for hours on a solid branch. The waiting was endless. Two more times David dropped a branch, and each time Mama Bear charged below. Her wrath escalated—faster, angrier, a little more out of control. Was she truly lying in wait for them? It appeared to be so. This bear was smart, and god help them, they inadvertently had come between her and her cubs.

Heavy, thick, snowflakes landed on the tip of David's nose. He looked up into a palate of solid white. Heavy clouds had settled in and opened, dumping down snowflakes. And lots of them. The dim light appeared to give way to twilight. It wouldn't be long before complete darkness surrounded them. David shivered. He knew if they stayed up here any longer they'd freeze, and any hope of finding their way home tonight would be lost. David swallowed. His cracked, dry lips stung from the light wind that brushed through the trees. Then, one by one, he lowered himself down a branch. A sharp sting seared his bare hands, even his feet, making each step excruciating.

"Where are you going?" Rose's voice shook. Was it fear or cold? He didn't know. When he looked up in the dim light, he could see her vague outline and firm grip on the branch above her.

"It's been quite a while since she last charged; I think she might be gone."

"Drop another branch first. Please, David. Wait for Daddy. He'll come looking for us, won't he?"

Instead of answering, David broke off another branch and dropped it. He prayed for help and held his breath as he watched the branch fall. Nothing happened—no aftershock or fiery attacking Mama bear. Only a light whistle of wind rustled the brush surrounding the tree. David glanced up; he was sure he saw Rose's hopeful expression. "Dad should start looking for us now. I'm climbing down to get my gun; you stay here until I call you."

"Be careful, she might be waiting."

David struggled to hold onto each branch and slide down, each step slow and painful. Beads of sticky sweat dripped down his underarms. Every hair on his head sizzled against his tender scalp as he stared at the heavy darkened bushes, searching for any sudden movement. This aggressive mother bear was devious and smart, and that made her dangerous. They encroached on her territory they were trespassers, which she perceived as a threat—a threat without a doubt she'd eliminate.

Hanging from the last branch, David searched the dim light for any movement. He listened hard over the echo of his heart pounding like drumbeats in his ear but could hear nothing except the whistle of the northern night wind.

He wanted to cry, he was scared, but David needed to hold it together for Rose. Where's Dad? In the light, Dad would find them but with the snow—the darkness? It'd be darn near impossible.

The unusually large snowflakes accumulated on the ground, covering the bushes in a blanket of white. David's breath fogged in front of him. It was getting cold, and he knew it would get a lot colder yet.

David's hands slipped and he landed hard on both feet, shooting razor sharp pistons up both his legs. He didn't think; he used the pain to roll on his side and swept the snow away as he searched for the now hidden shotgun. He didn't know if it were panic or relief when his finger touched the metal. He snatched up that shotgun and pulled the hammer back. He jumped to his feet, taking aim, and turned in a wide circle. He held his breath as he listened, no rustling, no warning growl. David released a shaky breath. His eyes blurred just as his knees weakened. With a shaky hand, he swiped his eyes. Suck it up. Now's not the time to lose it.

"Rose, climb down. We need to get out of here."

David listened as the branches rustled above him. He could hear Rose sniff and grunt as she slowly made her way down. And he kept watch, shuffling in a wide circle, around and around.

"Is the bear gone?"

David's teeth chattered, and it hurt to speak. "I don't know. She may not be far."

Rose landed with a thud and rolled in the snow. "I'm so cold. What are we going to do?"

David squeezed his eyes shut. He didn't want to be in charge. Where was Dad?

"David, it's dark. What should we do?"

"I don't know! We can't just start walking. It's dark. I can't see the way. And the snow's getting heavier."

He couldn't think; the panic was shaking his insides. And it was Rose's soft, muffled cry behind him that helped him pull it together. She was depending on him, and he needed to look out for her. A tear slipped out and trailed down his cheek. "I'll start a fire. Clear a spot, under that old Cedar—gather some branches—anything dry. Don't worry Rose, Dad will find us. He'll be looking now." He wouldn't look at her.

David cradled the shotgun in the crook of his arm while Rose cleared a spot under the large cedar. The draped branches created a shelter from the wind and falling snow.

David said nothing else to Rose. She must have known they were going to have trouble starting a fire. He had no matches. With a jackknife and string in his pocket, he could string a bow and rub a branch to create friction. If the wood were dry it'd be easy, but it was wet from the month-long rain.

A branch snapped and something rustled in the bush to David's left. David's stomach pitched, sending every nerve into a tailspin. His reaction was instinctive; take aim, pull the hammer back, as he poised a shaky finger on the trigger. Then he did a hard blink for a split second, to clear his foggy vision. He was confused in the dark. Where'd it come from again? He guessed, firming his stance slow and steady, and started to squeeze the trigger. A beam of light flickered through the trees, brighter — closer, coming right toward them.

"David! Rose!" Their names were shouted. The shotgun slid from his shaky hold toward the ground. Tears spilled down David's icy cheeks. He shouted, "Dad, Dad, over here!"

A bright light again flickered from the bush. It was Dad holding a lantern. He was with Uncle Patrick, and they were riding Sparky and Blue their two draft horses. Rose bolted straight to their father as he climbed off Blue. David's knees gave way, and he sank to the ground. He bowed his head. He couldn't stop the flow of stinging tears and wondered how angry his father would be. A man didn't cry.

But it was a strong, supportive hand that touched his shoulder, strong, loving arms that pulled him up. "It's okay David, you're safe. Rose said there was a bear."

David looked up at his father and buried his head against his chest. "She kept us pinned all day, with her cubs." His father didn't admonish him. He didn't get mad at him. He took David's gun helped him onto the saddle and mounted behind him.

"You spent the day up a tree?"

"Yes. Dad, I'm sorry, I didn't get the goose." His Dad surrounded him with his arms and held the reigns, before chirping and turning Blue, a gleaming white horse, around.

"It's okay David. What's important is you and Rose are safe. You can tell me all about it at home. I know you're scared. But you did good."

The End

Recipe for Christmas Goose

Ingredients

1 fresh or frozen 12 – 15 pounds goose
Salt and freshly ground black pepper
2 medium carrots, scrubbed and cut in half
2 stalks celery, cut in half
1 head garlic
1 bunch fresh thyme sprigs
1 bunch fresh sage
1 medium onion
10 sprigs flat-leaf fresh parsley
1 bay leaf
1 teaspoon whole black peppercorns
1/2 cup dry white wine
1 tablespoon organic butter or margarine

Directions

Heat oven to 400 degrees. Rub thawed goose inside and out with sea salt. Rinse well and pat dry. Trim as much of the excess fat as possible from the opening of the cavity. Remove first and second joints of the wings, and set aside for making the stock.

With the point of a sharp knife, prick the entire surface of the goose skin, being careful not to cut into the flesh. Fold the neck flap under the body of the goose, and pin the flap down with a toothpick. Generously sprinkle the cavity with salt and pepper, and insert carrot halves, celery-stalk halves, garlic, thyme, and sage. Tie legs together with kitchen twine. Generously sprinkle outside of the goose with salt and pepper, and place it, breast-side up on a wire rack that's inside a large roasting pan.

Roast goose in oven until it turns a golden brown, about 1 hour.

Then reduce heat to 325. With a baster, remove as much fat as possible from the roasting pan every 30 minutes. Roast until the goose is very well browned and thermometer inserted into a breast, not touching a bone, registers 180 degrees.

Prepare goose stock, which will be used when making the gravy and the dressing. Trim and discard any excess fat from the wing tips, neck, and giblets, and place them in a small stockpot. Add 3 carrot halves, 3 celery-stalk halves, 1 onion half, parsley, bay leaf, peppercorns, and enough water to cover the bones and vegetables about 2 litres of water. Place the stockpot over high heat, and bring to a boil, then simmer for 2 hours. Strain stock.

Remove goose from oven, and transfer it to a cutting board. Let the goose stand 15 to 20 minutes.

Meanwhile, prepare the gravy. Pour off all the fat from roasting pan, and place the pan over high heat. Pour in wine, and cook, stirring up any brown bits with a wooden spoon until the cooking liquid is reduced by half. Add 2 cups goose stock, and cook, stirring until the liquid is again reduced by half. Season with salt and pepper to taste. Stir in butter or margarine, and cook until slightly thickened.

Chapter Six

PIES FOR PERSONAL USE *by Genevieve McKay*

What most people have generally assumed, and what was perpetuated by the few unauthorized hacks who attempted to write about my part in that awkward period in the evolution of our species, was that first Christmas in the year of The Change must have been a bleak one.

I'll admit that as my head was being painfully bounced down the frozen marble steps of my childhood home and I was dragged by my heels through the muddy remnants of the rose garden by my parents' ever-efficient butler Jeffers, I had a few moments of astonished hurt, anger and self pity. I had guessed that my parents had considered me something of an oddity in our household but never, until that moment when my grandmother's death dissolved her protection over me, had I fathomed the depths of their hatred.

I had little time to feel sorry for myself before my ample bosomed mother was headed down the steps towards me like an ogre, her ample arms full of porcelain vases which she proceeded to hurl at me along with every insult known to man, or beast.

My dear father was there as well, waving his cane over his head in a wild farewell salute and urging me to say a final goodbye to my inheritance and to please never darken their doorstep again.

Due to the shouting there was no shortage of witnesses to later recount this tale in many a History. However, this is the point where the story and the truth must part ways. For instead of holing myself up in a dumpster and bemoaning my fate as has been written, I indeed saw that this was the first moment of my freedom.

Almost as soon as my body hit the sidewalk I had mourned the loss of my grandmother, detached myself from my old life and had begun to cast around for my next step. I was soon brushing myself off as best I could and limping my way down the street with my battered hands stuffed into my overcoat and my nose snuffling to find the sweet warm air currents of Prosperity.

Although I didn't have any money or any prospects, I did in fact possess something much better. While the majority of my latent talents were still emerging I had discovered a year or so ago that I had a sort of sixth sense where my betterment was concerned. This was one of the many things that my parents found unnatural about me. I was a natural hunter who could always find what was lost, or hiding, and seemed to attract to myself exactly what I needed.

It came to me in that moment with the dusty smell of dried roses and a soft touch on my cheek. I inhaled eagerly and began to trot along, casting back and forth for scent with my chest puffed out and my nose quivering high in the air. I must have looked very silly in those early days before I learned to track with finesse but I don't think in that moment that I cared.

All of a sudden the sweet rose smell turned into fresh bread baking and the next moment I was automatically trotting into a little café that had a giant coffee bean in a sombrero parked outside. Eagerly I threw open the door and leapt inside as though I expected my destiny to be waiting there with open arms.

There were only a few people in the café but they all looked up to stare disinterestedly at me for a moment before going back to their books and laptops. Both the rose smell and bread smell had dropped away completely and I felt my confidence turn into awkward embarrassment.

I must have looked a wreck because the waitress clucked at me sympathetically and beckoned toward an empty seat which I accepted gratefully.

"You must have quite the story to tell" she said, taking in my disheveled appearance. She set a cup of steaming coffee down in front of me.

"I'm off work in a few minutes. Stick around and we'll talk."

Everything was warm and safe inside and I took a moment to breathe and count my good fortune. A few moments later the waitress slipped into the seat beside me. She had untied her hair and it fell in loose waves down her back. She stared at me for a long moment with large, serious eyes as if coming to terms with some internal decision.

Finally she nodded.

"I believe that you'll do, but tell me about yourself first. Were you run over by a street cleaner?"

I laughed, a strange barking sound that was harsh to my ears. I cleared my throat and pondered how to explain it to her.

"My family kicked me out" I said simply. "I have nowhere to go."

She gave me that long searching look again. "That's what I thought. Well maybe we can help each other out. I'm leaving for Rome in the morning. I don't know for how long exactly but my friend who was supposed to be staying at my apartment bailed out on me at the last minute. I wouldn't care except I have all these fish and all these tanks. I can't just ship them around to other people's houses and I'm supposed to be driving down to the airport hotel tonight. I know that it's crazy to even think of trusting my apartment to a stranger but I have a feeling about you somehow, and I really do need help."

I could not stop the grin from spreading over my face in amazement.

A few hours later I was trotting up the stairs to my new fifth floor apartment which had been fully paid with fish care and the promise of rent paid in the vague distant future.

Three days later when my reflection in the mirror did not look so battered and disreputable I got a hunch and followed my nose to Prelude, the gallery where my paintings had been quietly gathering dust for the last sixteen months. Martin must have seen me coming for he intercepted me at the door and hauled me into an office before I could say a word.

"We have a cheque for you Andrew" he hissed. "A big one. Your father came here to dispose of your paintings, but we told him that they had sold and that you already had the money. Your Grandmother, god rest her soul, would be rolling in her grave if she knew how those people have treated you."

"Here, take it", he said, thrusting an envelope into my hand. "Don't let them break you Andrew. You were always a strange one but your Grandmother loved you, and we all loved her. Bring more paintings when you can. We'll sell them. Now, get out of here before someone sees you."

And there it was. One moment destitute and the next moment I was a man with a roof over his head and money in his pocket, trotting down the street with my scarf bundled up past my ears and my breath blowing little jaunty smokestacks into the pre-Christmas air. Hardly the tragic figure that has been portrayed in popular literature.

Anyway, I digress. The first thing that I did once I knew that I had enough money to nestle safely in my apartment for the next four months was to go out and buy ridiculous amounts of food. Piles of food that suited my own nature, any food that I'd ever wanted and been denied.

I have to confess that I've always loathed holiday gatherings. My Grandmother was the only human related to me that I actually liked, so meeting with the entire hornets' nest of relatives was an extremely painful experience. There was no laughter in my parents' house, no warmth like the warmth that I read of in books or saw on the television. The grim scraping of cutlery on plates, the overcooked food, the stifling smell of meat, the unwanted presents, and, well, mostly the family itself actually, all conspired to make Christmas a dreary affair.

So for my first Christmas in my new life I decided to celebrate it exactly as nature intended me to. First I bought a giant bag of flour, followed by sugar and cinnamon, allspice and nutmeg, cloves and lemons. Then I bought apples and blueberries, peaches and blackberries, cranberries and pumpkins. Then I bought potatoes and yams, leeks and green onions, garlic and mushrooms. I bought everything I could fit into one cart and then I wrangled a small stock-boy into pushing another one around behind me so that I could fill that one too.

All in all it was a magnificent trip and when I finally got home I put on the apron I'd bought, that said Kiss the Chef, and got down to work.

Now, the food that was part of my mothers' stylish family gatherings all had one thing in common: physical perfection. They may have been dry and tasteless, they may have been stingy on the fruit, but my mother insisted that each pie should look good enough to serve the Queen should she happen to drop by unannounced for Christmas dinner. All pies must be uniform, she said. All pies must be slightly browned but not too brown, and all pies must have fluted crusts with three identical slashes like claw marks in the exact centre.

I'd like to say that I broke completely free from my constricting past and danced around the house tossing flour over my shoulder in wild abandon, but alas, I was not yet far enough away from my beginnings for that. I still craved a bit of order, just my own order.

I did however make one new rule for pies. Pies must be enjoyed beyond measure.

Anyway, the pies that I made on that night were perfect. They were not too big and not too small. They were just the size where you could pick them up with both hands and eat them like that if you wanted to. They were wonderful. Their crusts may have been too thick in some places and too thin others, and I may have carved my initials into each little top crust, but if you could have smelled the apartment that night you would never have wondered if I had had a merry Christmas or not. The sweet fruit pies! The rich earthy vegetable pies. The aroma of cinnamon, nutmeg and cloves filling up every room like music, wrapped around me like a warm blanket. It was beautiful. When it was all done and every pie sat in its place cooling, I took off my apron and sat back to assess my situation.

It was a stunning amount of food, and of course I couldn't possibly begin to eat it all myself even with my unnatural appetite. I could freeze some for later, I thought. What I really wanted to do was find a fitting way to use them to celebrate my new life. A way that suited my nature. The bridge of my nose began to tickle and I felt my hackles rise with excitement. Of course! The idea burst into my head fully formed.

I made my second rule for pies. Pies must be shared.

I skipped around the room triumphantly, throwing on my overcoat and winding my scarf around my neck. It was easy to wrap up some of the best pies in canvas and tie them up nicely with a bit of string. In the end I had six tempting pies all wrapped up like little presents. More than enough for my purposes.

My apartment was an exceptional one when you consider that the rent was free, but it was not in what you call a high end, or even middle end area. It did not take long at all for my jaunty steps to take me past the nice Christmas shops to the more shabby shops and then past those to houses that were crowded close together with only the occasional cheery lights blazing in the windows. Past those still further and I got to the place I needed. Dark streets lapped by the water, old boats creaking against the docks, the patter of water rats out looking for dinner. Everything was cold and wet, no cheer. The perfect place for pies.

It wasn't long before she arrived and for a brief moment I wondered if I were making a mistake. She was much different than I remembered. She was thin as a reed, wrapped in a threadbare coat that left her soft white throat exposed to the cold. She wasn't much more than a child really and she wasn't paying attention to where she was going. She stumbled on the rain-slick ramp for a moment and I caught sight of her face in the street lamp. Her eyes were puffy from crying and her skin was pale and stretched from bad living. I could smell the stench of alcohol coming from her and even in the darkness I could see a fresh bruise marking her cheek.

She lurched past me, so close that I could have reached out and grabbed her, but I waited until she had sat down almost right beside me and slid down the dock railing to sit huddled in her coat, her face buried in her hands.

"Hello Christina" I said, as gently as I could. "Would you care for a pie?"

She went dead still and then she looked up wearily with a face full of sad resignation.

"Don't bother, she said dully, "If you've come to kill me then just get it over with. I really don't care."

I stared at her in surprise, considering. To give myself a moment I laid a red cloth on the ground and set out the pies in a circle and unclasped a thermos of hot chocolate. I looked up to see her watching me without interest.

"How old are you now?" I asked

She squinted at me blearily with eyes that looked about a hundred years old. " Just piss off" she said listlessly. "Whatever you're selling I don't want it. Go away."

"I'm here to help you Christina." I said gently. "If you'll let me."

"Twelve," she said after a long moment. "I'm twelve. Are you planning to drag this out much longer? I know it's a Christmas thrill for you but I'd be ever so grateful if you'd just get it over with. "

I unwrapped a pie, a blueberry one loaded with cinnamon, and pushed it towards her. She looked away but I saw her swallow reflexively as the smell hit her nose.

"Go on," I said, "I made it for you."

She kept her head turned away but I could see her nose working.

"You've drugged it, "she said bitterly. "You don't want to kill me, you want to kidnap me and sell me. Great."

"Christina, I said gently, you of all creatures know that it's not drugged. Use your nose."

I saw her eyes widen with shock, and fear, and maybe a hint of excitement.

"Oh, " she said suddenly, "It's YOU. Why didn't you say so in the first place?" Her hand reached out and picked up the pie.

"Do you remember the first time Christina? When you were a baby? I was just a teenager myself

114

when I saw you with your mom at the grocery store. You had just bitten one of you brothers and your mother had slapped you and called you a monster. You didn't cry, you didn't even look at her. You were watching me with those strange blue green eyes, strange eyes that I'd never seen on anyone except my own face in the mirror. And that's when I knew. I knew that there were more of us. That I wasn't alone.

"What are we then?" She asked around a mouthful of potato.

I looked down to see that all but two pies were gone. She was quick.

"I don't know exactly. But we're not evil, and we're not monsters. It's true that I can leap higher and have better senses than most people, but I don't kill for fun and I don't want to hurt things."

She looked at me considering for a moment and then shrugged. "Well, I don't have any place to live now and you make kick-ass pies so I guess I'd better come home with you."

She dismissed my excited smile and outstretched hand with a small motion of her head. "The rules are though that you don't touch me and that I have nice clothes to wear and that I get to go to school. I have plans for my future and I don't need anyone messing them up. Okay?"

"Fine," I said, "but then that means no more drinking alcohol until you're at least 20 and no wandering around at night by the docks taking food from random strangers."

She narrowed her eyes at me and worked hard to fight back a smile.

"Deal," she said, ignoring my outstretched hand. "We have a deal. Now, let's go home. I haven't had a shower in days."

I pretended to groan but couldn't help doing a little hop-skip of joy as I packed up the last crumbs from dinner and we set off towards home. Welling up in my heart was such a feeling of gladness as I'd never known. I had the beginnings of a family and I was free. It was indeed a Christmas miracle.

Recipe for Blueberry Pie

Okay, here is a quick and dirty version of the blueberry pie filling (this actually works for any berry filling, and is really good). No measurements; pies are meant to be artistic!

Put a chunk of butter into a saucepan and let it start to bubble. Add a couple of generous splashes of berry juice (whichever flavour you like).

Sift in a spoonful of cornstarch. Add the cornstarch slowly so that it doesn't clump up, and keep stirring. It's going to thicken fast, so have extra berry juice on hand just in case it needs more liquid.

Add brown sugar (as much as you like) and a pinch of salt.

Then add the berries and reduce to a low heat.

Stir in cinnamon and nutmeg, and a splash of rum if you like.

Let it all bubble together until it is a rich, thick, texture and then spoon into pie shell.

Cover with other pie and put into the oven to brown for 15 minutes or so (whatever it takes to bake the crust).

Use whatever crust recipe you like, or use the pre-made stuff.

For extra decadence don't forget to brush some melted butter over the top crust just before it comes out of the oven, and to sprinkle some sugar over it.

Let it bake for 5 more minutes and then it's ready to go!

Chapter Seven

TIT FOR TAT *by W.J.Merritt*

The small apartment building didn't even have an automatic door. Connie saw the old woman struggling to get her walker through. Running to the door, Connie pulled it open. "How are you, Mrs. Driscoll?"

The woman grunted and gave the walker a shove. "Why should you want to know?" Her voice was gravelly, but strong.

Smiling, "Oh, Mrs. Driscoll, we have this same conversation every day."

"So why keep asking?" The limp on her right side more obvious as she tried to speed her getaway.

"Here, let me help you with those groceries."

"Don't need any help. Manage just fine on my own."

"That is obvious, Mrs. Driscoll," Connie said reaching for the three bags on the walker, as Mrs. Driscoll fumbled in the worn leather bag she was never without, looking for her keys.

The hallway had no heat and the cold winter air moved around them like a moist fog. Connie wondered how warm she was in her thin coat.

"I'll take those bags." Mrs. Driscoll reached for the bags.

"That's okay; I'll just set them on the cupboard for you." Connie moved deftly around the woman and entered a place she had never been invited.

The apartment was clean and there was a lingering aroma of the past. Connie set the bags on the cupboard and took a better look. The furniture was old and worn. The coffee table, all the tables were adorned with lace doilies. "Did you make the doilies?"

The old woman finished mumbling something Connie was glad she hadn't heard and said "Yes."

"I would love to learn how to make them. Would you teach me?"

"Nobody tats anymore and you young people don't care about it."

Connie looking into the distance, said, "Nannie said it was a dying art. We did all kinds of crafts; knitting and crocheting, sewing, everything but tatting. She was going to teach me to tat but..."

"But what...?" Was this a tad of interest from the old lady?

"She died last year. We never got to the tatting." Connie moved toward the door. "See you later, Mrs. Driscoll."

No reply.

Connie moved to the door across from Mrs. Driscoll's and opened it. Looking around her small apartment she felt cold. Bare, sparse but trendy furniture, with unique lamps and pictures met her sight. No doilies. No smell. No feeling. Maybe moving to New York was not one of her brightest choices.

She thought about the elusive dream to be a well-known editor in a big publishing house. That meant going back to school. Not what she wanted to do. She needed to figure out what she wanted to do pretty fast, this job as a shoe salesperson wasn't the way she saw herself; when she grew up.

Enough dawdling, she gave herself a shake. She had to get back to work and needed to get a bite to eat. Working so close to home was great, even if this was just till something better came along; just something to do till she grew up.

She threw together a tuna sandwich and grabbing two of the whipped shortbread cookies, Nannies recipe; the only Christmas baking she had done, so far. She flicked the switch leaving the light on; it would be dark when she came home.

The afternoon dragged. Not because there weren't any customers, there were, but because she was getting paid today. She was buying her Christmas tree and decorations; more important, the gifts. The other tenants in the building would be surprised and they would never guess she was Santa. Christmas was the best time of the year. Nannie loved Christmas. She shone at Christmas. She was the one person Connie had ever known whose love was unconditional. She would decorate to the max and there was lots to eat. Christmas Eve they played games and ate and laughed and finally watched 'It's A Wonderful Life' or 'A Christmas Carol'.

"Connie." Connie looked towards her boss.

"When you have finished cleaning and vacuuming, before you leave, I want to see you in my office."

"Okay." What now. Her low back was aching, she just wanted to go home grab a couple of Tylenol and get on with her evening plans... She'd had this job for three weeks and could not seem to please the owner. The only compliment she had received was on the Christmas decorating she'd done. Unfortunately, she knew it herself; she was more-artistically-talented in decorating than selling shoes. She wasn't fussy about shoes. Give her a pair of flats and she was happy. Oh well, it wasn't the stiletto's that were going to do the cleaning in here.

She nudged the vacuum a little further into the crowded closet with her foot and closed the door firmly. Wiping her hands on her slacks she knocked on the manager's office door, patted her hair and was allowed to enter.

"There you are." Her boss was shuffling papers around her desk in an obvious gesture of allowing her thoughts to reach her mouth.

Her boss looked up and met Connie's gaze. This couldn't be good. "I don't believe in beating around a bush." Connie could attest to that statement.

"I am going to have to let you go."

"No. You can't!" As the words sunk in Connie felt her chest tighten. She felt prickles under her armpits, never had she been 'let go'.

Her bosses eyebrows lifted, her head changed position, ever so slightly. "I can't?"

"I need this job. I am buying my Christmas stuff tonight. Is there something wrong with my work? I am always on time. What have I done wrong?" She felt the heat on her face, fear in her head, and a hole in the solar plexus of her body. All the emotions that produced tears. Her most feared curse.

"Please, reconsider." Connie searched her mind for words to win her case. Nothing. She would not cry in front of this woman.

The tears were there; rimming her eyes. She blinked them away.

"I realize that Christmas is not a good time, no time is a good time to lose your job but it's just not working. I just don't feel at ease with leaving you alone in the store. Little things but I need to mesh with my employee. You have good attributes but selling is not one of them. Sales are down. That's the bottom line." She shuffled some more papers on her desk, bending over; she set the loud, gaudy purse on the desk with a thud.

"What I am willing to do is let you work till the end of the month. Think about it. You will still have Christmas Eve, Christmas Day and Boxing Day off. Work Tuesday at the regular time."

"But..."

"I am sorry but this decision is final. Now, let's get out of here." The hands gripping her bag were turning white; her usually expressionless face was grimacing. Her voice hard. Final.

The wind was cold and snow was curling down to be packed on the sidewalk by shoppers. Connie moved deeper into her winter coat and walked. Continuing through the hurrying people, Christmas displays, even the bright lights of the Big Apple didn't penetrate the maze of thoughts swirling in her head.

Now what? Her eyes stung from the icy wind and the tears, threatening to break their barrier. She'd been just coasting through life on auto-pilot since her grandmother's death. Dealing with it but not dealing with it. She missed Nannie so much.

Connie saw herself in a window and didn't much care for what she saw. Her dark eyes looked overbearing on her pale skin. Wisps of chocolate brown hair were framed by her toque. In the reflection she was shrinking into her coat, into herself.

Nannie, what am I going to do? She listened but heard only people laughing, cars honking. Lots of people but she was so alone.

She longed to have Nannie here. Giving her advice, encouraging her to move on, through or over it. It's how it had been since her parent's death when she was eight.

I should never have come here. How stupid am I? I should go home.

Thoughts like ping pong balls, hit at all the corners of her mind. The pain behind her eyes blinding. The back ache was all around and even into her abdomen. I have to get home. Her thoughts hammering inside her head were making her feel sick. Faint.

She had a small trust fund from her parents. Her grandmother's cute little house in a small town, sat empty, not selling. It would take all of that and then some to go to live and go to college. She wanted a career. She had to prove to the people back home and more importantly, to herself. She would be a success on her own merits.

So, what do I want? As a knife-like slash of pain went through her head; she knew she needed to get home and lie down. She had tomorrow to worry about this. The street noises where only making her more confused.

As Connie entered the apartment building Mrs. Driscoll was coming out of her door. Connie wanted to just get in and go to bed. She didn't want Mrs. Driscoll to see her like this. Connie looked down, unwilling to meet the older woman's eyes as they passed. Connie had her key in her hand and she was reaching for the door handle when she was called to by Mrs. Driscoll.

"You okay?"

Connie looked up and starting to reply, when everything in line of sight disappeared. She swayed and crumpled.

Next thing she knew, two paramedics were standing over her and she was on the couch. She attempted to sit up but the pain was so intense she let her body move back into the position it had been in.

"So, you think she hit her head when she fell?" The attendant asked, checking her pulse.

"Young man, I know she hit her head." Mrs. Driscoll stated in her usual tone.

"She was out cold when we brought her in here." This male voice came from nearer the door. She had no idea who it was. "I'll see you later, Mrs. Driscoll."

In a tone of voice Connie had never heard her use, Mrs. Driscoll replied "Thanks for your help. I appreciate it."

"No worries. See you." The door closed behind him.

"Grab the gurney." Then the paramedic was talking to her. "Connie, do you think you can stand up and move to the gurney?"

Connie murmured softly, "I'm not sure. The pain is excruciating." Tears slid from the corner of her eyes. "If you just leave me it'll go away. It's a migraine. I don't need to go to the hospital; I just need to go to bed."

"In my opinion, after that fall and hitting your head, I think you should be checked out." He moved the coffee table and his partner rolled the gurney as close to her as he could.

Connie made a valiant effort to lift herself from her prone position but the pain was so bad she fell back onto the couch. "I can't. Just leave me here. I'll be okay in a while."

"No." Mrs. Driscoll said, "You are going and that's that."

She must have given the paramedics 'the look' because immediately Connie felt one on each side of her. "On three, we are going to stand you up and pivot you onto the gurney. One, two, and three…" She was up but was sure she was going to pass out again.

"I can't go to the hospital" Connie was crying; it felt like the pain was encasing her body everywhere. "Tomorrow is Christmas Eve. I haven't shopped. I haven't gotten groceries. What about work? Oh, Nannie would be so disappointed in me."

"Nonsense. Christmas is just another day. Your Nannie isn't here, she's dead. What is the name of the shoe store you work at? I'll let them know you won't be in tomorrow. Your health is what is important. Give me your keys and I'll lock up." Who was she to argue with the tone that ruled?

Connie kept her eyes closed and said, "The Shoe Inn. I had my keys in my hand. I need my purse." She tried to sit up and couldn't.

"Here's your purse. I have your keys. Off you go. I'll see you soon."

It was 11:20 Christmas Eve when the yellow cab dropped Connie off in front of her apartment. Her headache was controlled, with thanks to some good drugs and she was minus a kidney stone, also with deep appreciation.

The front door opened with the help of a walker and there was Mrs. Driscoll. "Get in here, child. You'll get your death of cold."

Might not be a bad idea. Connie caught, and shook herself, sorry for that thought. Nannie used to say "Listen to an old lady: without the bad, there isn't any way to measure the good."

Connie paid the cab driver and walked towards the open door, reluctant to go into her dreary, cold apartment.

Last Christmas, without Nannie had been hard enough. She hadn't done one single Christmassy thing, only cry. Things didn't look much different this year.

"When the hospital said you were on your way home I went in and turned up the heat. It won't be warm for awhile. Come on in, I have the water boiled for a cup of tea."

"Well, Mrs. Driscoll I am pretty tired. Would you mind if we skip tea?

"As a matter of fact, I do mind. Now you mind me and come have a nice cup of Chamomile herb tea and you'll sleep like a baby."

When Connie took in the determined stance of the woman and what looked like her unmovable walker, Connie decided that it would be easier to have the cup of tea.

Connie settled back into the comfortable old floral couch, put her head back and closed her eyes.

"I called that woman you work for and told her you wouldn't be in and she said not to bother coming back."

"Merry Christmas." Connie mumbled.

"I said you didn't need her job anyway." Mrs. Driscoll moved to the couch with the small tray of china, tea and the 'fixings'. "Here you go."

The two women sat sipping the hot tea in silence.

When Connie was finished she set down the fine bone china cup on its saucer. Standing up she said "I've got to get to bed. Thanks for the tea."

"I'll check on you in the morning." Mrs. Driscoll said. As the door closed Connie thought she heard the older woman say "Merry Christmas."

Yes, it was well after midnight. Connie opened the door to her apartment and was overwhelmed with the aroma of Gingerbread.

Her eyes went immediately to the small decorated tree on the coffee table. She knew it was real she could smell the pine scent. There were Christmas lights draped around the window. Christmas ornaments were placed around the living room. They were beautiful old ornaments; all the colors and fine workmanship of a bygone age.

The table was set elegantly in fine china, for three people. A note on the fridge said to please place the turkey in the oven by 8:00. Dinner would be at 4:00.

Connie couldn't fathom how this had all been done for her in the time she was in the hospital.

Connie opened her door and looked across the bare hallway. She wanted to knock on Mrs. Driscoll's door but couldn't see any light around it. All was in darkness and it was much too late. Mrs. Driscoll needed her sleep too.

Connie closed the door and locked it. Turning around she surveyed the glorious sight of Christmas that had been spread out for her. Oh, Nannie. I know you can see this. This beautiful Christmas gift I have received.

She moved over to the couch and sat down in front of the small, simply decorated tree. On the small skirt of the tree was an envelope. Connie reached for it and opened it. Inside was a coupon, 'This coupon entitles bearer to lessons on Tatting.'

Oh, Nannie, it is a Merry Christmas.

The End

Recipe for Whipped Shortbread Cookies

325% F   13-15 mins

I/2 lb. butter   1/2 lb. margarine

Soften over night

½ c. cornstarch   1 c. sifted icing sugar

3 c. sifted flour

Add dry ingredients to soften butter mixture and whip till like

whipped cream.

Drop by tsp. onto ungreased cookie sheet and top with a ½ of red

and green glazed cherries.

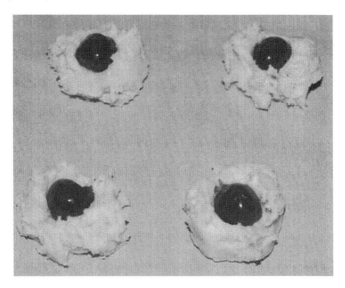

Chapter Eight

SCREWGE: THE REDEMPTION OF RABBI HAWKINS *by Jim Miller*

December, 1965

"Promote Hawkins?"

The Company Sergeant Major came out of his chair like a partly scalded bull moose. Part moose because that's what he looked like and part scalded because he had received a mug full of hot coffee into his lap. The mug, its work done, continued on its way until stopped by the scuffed hardwood floor of the office of the Officer Commanding, OC. The head of the little geisha figurine, who had once lived on the side of the mug, popped off to come to a dead halt a few inches away. The once inscrutable face peered unhappily upward.

"Hawkins! Always Hawkins. Just talking about him breaks my mug. And now you wanna promote thesonofa…"

The grouchy old bear blamed me for his smashed cup even though I wasn't present. Garrett's revered coffee mug had been purchased while he had been in Japan on R and R near the end of the Korean War. Word had it that his removal from Korea had been one of the non-negotiable demands from the North Korean representatives at the start of the armistice talks at Panmunjom.

And if I wasn't present, how did I come up with such an accurate account of the meeting? Johnny Doyle, a good buddy of mine, was the company runner that day. The company office was next door to the OC's office where the meeting was being held. Johnny, along with Mouse Clark, the six foot-two, mini-mountain who pretended he had typing skills sufficient to be the company clerk, had been listening through the paper thin walls. Between the two of them they remembered all the colourful details. Anyway, getting back to the meeting.

The nerve centre of Delta Company, First Battalion, the MacCammon Highlanders of Canada was holding its weekly meeting. Present were the Officer Commanding, Major Jason Charles; his second-in-command, Captain Fred Alfort and the Company Sergeant Major, W02, pronounced double-you-oh-two, Patrick Garrett. The first two were officers. Garrett was a soldier, what was known as an 'OR' or Other Rank. Major Charles called him Delta Company's enforcer and had often said, "Myself and Captain Alfort develop policy, Sarn't Major Garrett ensures that this abstraction manifests itself into reality."

You've seen Garrett's reaction to the mention of my name. and to be fair, I had been the proverbial thorn in his undercarriage. Major Charles was somewhat distanced from me and so had a calmer reaction.

"Hawkins a Lance Corporal...mmm. Care to explain the rationalization behind such an unconventional tactic, 2i/c?"

Captain Alfort nodded calmly. "It bears experimenting with, I'd say, Sir." He held up a little orange book, "an anthology of short stories for Canadian high schools …"

"If you'll excuse me, sir," Garrett pointed to the book, "But based on a book of stories we're gonna make Hawkins a Lance Corporal? You mean for us to give that shit-disturbing son of a gun a hook?"

Alfort smiled, he was quite used to Garrett's allergies to anything new, and to me.

"Go on, 2i/c, "said Major Charles. "Sounds intriguing." He glanced at his Company Sergeant Major and said, "Sarn't Major, haven't I heard you telling the NCOs to get the whole story before they… What's that colourful phrase you use?"

Garrett sat down and picked up the geisha's head and the now empty mug. "One second, Sir, just seeing if the beheaded could be reheaded."

Captain Alfort stepped in to pinch-hit, "getting all wrapped around the axle, I believe, sir."

"Right, so let's none of us get wrapped around the axle until it's necessary." He nodded to his second-in-command to go on.

"The synopsis; a small nation has just been overrun by the Romans and the conquering general has his hands full with rebels and malcontents trying to get the populace to rise up and give it another go. There is one, a local prophet…"

"Not JC by any chance, Fred?"

"No, sir."

Garrett said, "I hope not. There's no way this side of hell that I'd compare Hawkins with Jesus Christ."

"No. I agree with you, Sarn't Major, no comparison. Anyway, the Roman general calls for a

132

chat with the prophet and offers him a plum position, thinking that not only would that disarm him, but also they could use his influence over the rest of the insurgents."

Major Charles nodded, "set a thief to catch a thief in some roundabout way?"

Garrett growled, "No, sir, more like dress the fox up as a rooster and then shove him in to the henhouse. Hawkins with a hook, he'll be twice as bad as he is now."

There was silence in the room. Garrett looked out the window. Grunted to himself. Captain Alfort knew enough about his OC to wait. But Major Charles knew his Sergeant Major. He waited.

Garrett spoke first. "Gents, you are my bosses. And it's my job and duty to obey you." He looked at Alfort, then turned back to face the Major. "Both of you. But I also have a duty to offer my comments and advice." The OC nodded. Garrett went on, "So here's my advice in three words. Don't. Do. it."

Captain Alfort, the excellent judge of character that he was, maintained that, "If we bring Hawkins onside as a Lance Corporal, it'll turn him around. The rank will awaken a sense of responsibility in him."

Garrett disagreed, "the rank will offer greater opportunities for him to run rampant through the battalion."

The Major said, "both points have worth. However, he's been pretty much a renegade ever since his basic training. If we give him one stripe it may break the cycle. Maybe it will shake him up, turn him around…"

"If you're set on promoting him, there is a bright side, maybe it'll get him into jail faster, the slippery SOB," added the CSM.

Captain Alfort said, "Sarn't Major, there's a story going around the Battalion about a young soldier who was considered unsalvageable, until the RSM took him under his wing..."

The OC grinned, "I was a lieutenant then. Seem to remember that it wasn't so much take him under his wing as take him out back and explain military life to the... alleged shit disturber."

"Right, I get the picture, Sirs. But there's also the missing truck and the lobsters to worry about."

"CSM, surely you don't suspect Hawkins of that? The truck went missing from the military police vehicle compound. Hawkins had just been released from cells. He would have been under strict observation."

This time Garrett grinned, "And that's when Good ol' Rabbi Hawkins is the most dangerous. Yeah, we've been bugging Staff Sergeant Pritchett-Ingalls up in the Sergeants' Mess that he swiped the truck himself and has the lobsters in his freezer." He quit grinning and added, "Still, I'll bet a week's pay that Hawkins is involved in that stolen truck..."

He paused. No one jumped at the idea of easy money. "No takers, Gents?"

Captain Alfort shook his head, "No comment. But anyway, let's give this a try, shall we?"

Major Charles nodded, slowly, "Nothing further, CSM?"

"Once again, I caution you, sir. If you want a peaceful Christmas: Don't. Do. It."

***

While all that had been going on I had been in a more inhospitable spot on Camp Gagetown property. I was busy paying penance for the lobster run. Although busy didn't truly describe it.

"Rabbi, we're on a deadline!" E Squared yelled, looking at me and Ralphie already in down-tools mode. Other than the one or two half-hearted pokes at the snow mountain along the northwest corner of the parade square, we had done nothing. Even under the evil eye of Corporal Pet Monkey, the BOC, the Battalion Orderly Corporal, me and Ralphie hadn't exactly broken a sweat. Pet Monkey? Real name's Peter Monkman, but because he looked more chimpish-sapiens than homo sapiens that was the name we used. Not in his presence, of course.

After dire but empty threats, he had gone off to guzzle a few warm-ups in the Corporals' Mess. He had cautioned us that he would be back in a little while. He didn't mention how long he'd be away in hopes that we'd keep working. He's new and doesn't know Ralphie and me. It was bitterly cold, but we were clad in full winter kit; parkas, mukluks, heavy mittens, toques and scarves. And of course the work, if we had done any, would have kept us toasty warm.

I was sitting on a pile of snow eating a Mars bar and slugging back a coke. Ralphie sat beside me, chewing tobacco. We chewed, he spat, I swallowed and said, "Hear that. Ears says we got a deadline?"

Private Warren Sykes was Lieutenant Stoneman's batman. He was not called Elephant Ears or E Squared or 'Ears' because he had big ears. His ears were uncommonly small and quite tiny for his bulgy head. He got the name because he had hearing the way an eagle has telescopic vision. When we arrived in the Company we had been told that if an earthworm farted in a hurricane, Ears would not only hear it, but could tell you if it was male or female. No one who knew him thought it was a joke.

"Deadlines. Hah. I got eleven years in, leaves me fourteen more before I hit my deadline," Then he grinned at me, "My pension." He shrugged in his big green parka, "Shovel or sit and chew, it's all pensionable time, my good buddy."

"He ain't your good buddy," said E Squared.

I finished off my candy bar, crumpled the wrapper and tossed it toward the ditch where we were supposed to have been heaving the snow.

"Am I your good buddy, Ears?" said Ralphie.

"You're a jackass, Ralphie. And you, Hawkins, tossing chocolate bar wrappers around. Next thing you know we'll be out here picking up your garbage."

Ralphie grinned again and looked up at the gray, cloud-filled sky, "Snow'll be back tonight. Wrapper won't get picked up until next spring."

E Squared floundered toward us in his mukluks and bulky parka, a green Michelin Man, "It's littering, Rabbi. You should go and pick it up."

"Come Spring, Ralphie'll still be on defaulters. My bet is he'll be picking it up for me," I said.

E Squared finally arrived and stood close to me, "Good, he's a clown. Seven days, and all of them with that asshole."

I nodded, "Cruel and unusual punishment, E, that's for sure."

"Hey Ears, you're lucky you were just a minor accomplice," said Ralphie. He jerked a thumb at me. "Him being the Einstein of the criminal world, he got double."

"Shut up, Ralphie. Rab, I ain't blaming you. I got into this fair and square."

"You got into it because you're an idiot, Ears," said Ralphie, picking up and tossing a chunk of hard packed snow in my lap. "You too, Hawkins. What the hell came over you. Drive right down the main drag of camp and get picked up by a rookie meathead. All my training wasted." He shook his head and spat toward the ditch, dead centre into a patch of already tobacco-juice-stained snow, "I'm freezin'. Hope Pet Monkey doesn't spend all day in the Corporals' Mess."

I squinted up at the sky. "Yeah, this close to Christmas you think he'd go easy on us."

My watch said just gone two, but it was quite dark already -- it had not been bright all day -- and lights were flaring in the windows of the neighbouring barrack blocks, as if laughing at us for being outside on such a day. With any luck Pet Monkey wouldn't be able to see how much snow we had moved. Or hadn't moved. We sat in the afternoon gloom, huddled in our big coats, mitts, mukluks and our private thoughts. Mine concerned our snow mountain. I wasn't in favor of us shifting too much of this huge snow pile in front of us. And it had nothing to do with laziness; that mound of snow guarded a secret only I knew.

I was partly responsible for E Squared's situation, totally responsible for my own. E Squared was a native of New Brunswick, from Shediac, the lobster capital of the world; as he put it. Lobsters were what got us into this mess. Me and E Squared, not Ralphie.

The first week of December we had been caught doing a midnight run in a stolen army vehicle to Shediac, the aforementioned lobster capital of the world. We had traded three hundred cases of Army rations to a lobster fisherman for ten dozen lobsters. The lobsters were destined for a Delta Company party. We made it all the way back to camp, and then a few hundred yards from our hidey-hole, we were nabbed by a military policeman. Yes, as Ralphie said, a rookie cop. Once the truck was sequestered in the military police compound, we spent a few hours in cells and then were released to the custody of the Duty Sergeant.

I was lucky enough to re-swipe the truck and lobsters less than three hours after our release. The minor accomplice was not around when I needed him, so the deed was done by the lone lobsternapper. I drove the truck out of the MP compound, and as I cruised past the parade square saw it was being cleared by some engineers with ploughs. They were piling the snow up at the far end of the parade square. A few days before the lobster run, we had had another blizzard and the parade square and the camp were under at least four feet of snow.

I had driven the truck down a trail near the gym, parked it and went off to supper. After supper, I went back and checked on the ploughs. The crews had called it a night. I snuck over and looked at the machines. I felt confident I could operate one with a bit of practice. The controls didn't look that much different from those on a Armoured Personnel Carrier.

During the time I was ploughing and burying, two military police jeeps went by on patrol. One stopped, as did my heart. But after looking me over, it sped off. I had parked the truck near the pile, then cleared a small canyon in the snow pile and drove the truck in there and buried it. I didn't finish burying the truck and the lobsters until three in the morning.

After the summary trial where the absence of any overwhelming lobster evidence was not taken into consideration, we commenced our punishment tour. I got fourteen days confinement to barracks, which included days of shoveling snow. Ears being a minor accomplice got seven days. Minor accomplice my ass. Hell, he stole the three-quarter ton truck. He loaded the rations while I dickered with a supply Corporal at the Camp commissary. And it was his uncle who supplied the lobsters. And wouldn't you just know it. Our punishment was to move the truck-hiding-snow pile off the side of the parade square and into the ditch running along that side of the square. If we got too ambitious, we'd expose the missing truck. I couldn't have that.

Sitting there on the snow pile, we had shifted our conversation to the relative intelligence of military police in general when a voice yelled, "Rabbi! Hawkins! Hey Rab!"

I stood up, shifted a few feet over to where I could see and sauntering right down the middle of the snow-choked road came Barker, first name Tom, but never used. He was just Barker. He had on a red ski jacket, jeans, and his army mukluks along with his army issue black dress gloves. On his head he wore a yellow and red toque.

"Rabbi? You're wanted up at the company office, Sergeant Farley said to report ASAP, garrison dress, winter, number twos."

That meant battledress tunic, long-sleeved green shirt and tie, kilt, brown hose, puttees, black boots, leather sporran and balmoral or scottish-styled hat with pom-pom on top. Luckily, I had that all set to go. Being a defaulter meant having to report in a variety of uniforms while attending compulsory parades that started at 0600 hours and went through to the 2200 hour Staff parade. In situations like that a supply of clean, pressed uniforms was a necessity.

"What's up?"

"Went up to get my pass for the weekend, and he gave me the message. Johnny was on his way to find you. Whispered, Rabbi's getting made up..." Barker shrugged, "some kind of joke?"

"Made up? Hah! One hundred percent pure boondoggle. No one's gonna promote Rabbi. Nobody never," said Ralphie.

Based on my recent track record I agreed with him. I shook my head, "Couldn't be. Doyle's putting you on."

Barker shook his head, "nope, sounded straight. Rabbi's getting made up. Plain as day."

Ears said, "don't matter if it's true or not. You better get your ass up to the office."

And with no wiser words to be said, I accompanied Barker back to our building. I flung my uniform on, and as usual my puttees rebelled. Two attempts on each leg but finally they were wrapped on over the boot tops and part way up my leg the required distance and with the little knot off to one side as is directed in battalion dress regs. I set off to find out what this was all about. I entered the company office and there were Doyle and Mouse Clark gabbing away. Mouse, huge behind his desk and typewriter. Johnny sitting on the mail table swilling coffee. He slid off the table. "Rabbi..."

"Hawkins!"

Overruled by a larger voice, Johnny hopped back on his roost.

"Sir?"

"My office. Now."

"Sir." And as I stood at attention in the doorway he said, "get in here."

I get in here-d, marched forward and halted two paces in front of Garrett's desk. Lying on his blotter was the mug and the geisha's head. An April Fools joke that involved him hiding the Sergeant Major's mug, cost Corporal Wilbur five days of Company Orderly Corporal. From that incident we learned it was safer to steal the Battalion Colours than to mess with Hop Sing, as we called her.

"Too bad, CSM, you've broken Hop Sing?"

"She ain't no Hop Sing, Hawkins. That's that dopey cook on Bonanza. That..." He pointed toward the carnage, "is a Japanese geisha girl. I've had her... Never mind. You are going in front of the OC. And while what's to come may be a shock, unbelievable and whatever else you want to say about it, its going to happen. Once done there, we'll come back here." He paused, shaking his head.

Maybe it's true. Maybe I was getting made up... but it couldn't be. There was absolutely no reason why that would be on my radar even during the most optimistic of my daydreams.

Garrett looked at his watch, grunted at it as if it were lying, then stood up. "Showtime, Lad. Follow me." We ended up in front of the OC's office. Garrett knocked and a voice bid us enter.

My usual routine when in front of the OC was to stand in front of the Major's desk while Garrett read out the list of alleged sins. As in baseball, my number of at-bats produced more strikeouts than homers; and I took my punishment, either financial or confinement to barracks. But overall, my legal record of defending myself was markedly more successful than many of my peers. Some appearances I argued to a standoff and the Major, being a believer in the concept of reasonable doubt, would dismiss the case. Generally speaking, being who I was, and with my rep, guilty was a given. Not that I ever walked in like a lamb to the slaughter. I had discovered that a good legal argument could often result in a reduced sentence.

Today was different. I marched forward, halted, saluted and that's when it hit me: a criminal entered without a headdress: I was still wearing mine. Garrett hadn't ordered me to remove it. The Major was wearing his balmoral and he stood up, returned the salute and came around the desk. I saluted and he returned my salute. Whatever this was about, I wasn't being charged.

"Good afternoon, Hawkins."

"Afternoon, sir."

"It is my pleasure, Private Hawkins, to promote you to Lance Corporal LQ..." He paused, "You understand LQ?"

"Yes sir, lacking qualification."

"Correct. And as you may be aware, the rank of lance corporal is one a company commander can confer upon a private under his command who was lacking both time and rank and the junior NCO course, such a person as yourself."

It was true. I was about to become a lance corporal. An NCO. Of course, it was an unpaid rank, but it was a rank.

Reviewing this situation much later, I wondered just when my attitude on the military world had shifted. Formerly, I'd been among the criminal element of the Battalion. Suddenly I was a member of the Battalion's leadership infrastructure. When did that shift occur? Was it as the OC slipped the Lance Corporal's brassard with that one stripe onto my arm? Was that the moment that I slid across that invisible line from law-breaker to law-enforcer? Did the change from law-evading to law-abiding occur in Garrett's office? Or did it happen as I walked down the road after leaving his office?

"Just so you understand, Lance Corporal." And there it was, Major Charles had actually called me Lance Corporal.

"The rank is provisional and can be revoked at any time based on conduct prejudicial to good order and discipline."

"Right, sir. I understand. It's mine as long as I walk the line."

"Good."

"Congratulations, Lance Corporal Hawkins," said Major Jason Charles as he shook my hand.

"Thank you, sir."

"Yes, Well done, Lance Corporal Hawkins," said the Company 2i/c, Captain Fred Alfort, from his position at the side of the Major's desk. He gave me a grin, "Kind of an early Christmas present. From the rear of the room came a grunt from Sergeant Major Garrett, the Company Sergeant Major and the one man who saw me as a shit disturber. Thankfully I did have an ally. Captain Alfort saw an intelligent, sharp soldier who cut corners, but was also a natural leader. His words, not mine. A first rate assessment, if I do say so myself. A fine judge of character that Captain Alfort.

I saluted, turned with a near-perfect about turn and marched sharply out of the company commander's office. Just by being promoted my drill had improved.

Garrett and I re-convened in his office where the atmosphere was distinctly anti-Lance Corporal Yours Truly.

"You'll be on the Spring Junior NCO Course, Hawkins… That is, if you're still packing that hook."

"Yes, sir."

"And for now you'll be a company supernumerary."

I knew that meant that I wasn't going to be given a section second-in-command role. Which was fine. Being a Lancejack without portfolio gave me more room to sort out the company. I realized that I had a ton of work to do. For some time now it was a feeling I had that Garrett had been slipping. It didn't occur to me that any sign of disciplinary slippage on Garrett's part was simply my learning the ins and outs of a battalion's rules and regulations. I'd figured out the shortcuts and played it close to the edge. Now I was eyes wide-open at the idea that the time had come to

144

shut some of those loopholes. It never occurred to me that I might still need them. What I saw was a leadership cadre throughout the entire battalion that had fallen asleep at the wheel. Clearly, it was my duty to demonstrate to all concerned that law and order was back with a vengeance. And it came dressed as Lance Corporal Hawkins. I left Company Headquarters wearing my Lance Corporal brassard and set a course to the tailor shop to get my stripes sewn on both sleeves.

I had no idea that my first opportunity at cracking down on the criminal populace of the Battalion was sauntering toward me unaware that a new sheriff was on the job.

"Hey, Rabbi, how's it going?"

"Yeah, looking good Rab!"

"What did you say, lad?"

"Said hello, Rab. Why, what's up?"

It was clear that my Lance Corporal hook had taken over my brain. Think about it. One minute I'm defaulter Hawkins doing fourteen days, the next I'm a Lance Corporal threatening to toss one of my peers into jail. Or ex-peer. I had mentioned earlier that the Battalion needed a wake-up call. And wouldn't you know it? The alarm just went off. Opportunity knocks.

I spun to face one, "And you, Sather, did I just see you throw away a butt. That's littering. Go and pick it up. Now."

"Hey, Hawkins, settle down," said the first guy as Sather moved off to dig through the snow.

I shifted back to face him, one finger pointing to the Lance Corporal brassard on my arm, "Did my brother join?"

"Hey, way to go…"

"Never mind. What's with the Hawkins bit? For your information, Private Johnson, it's Corporal to you and you too, Sather." I moved my hand up again and pointed at the Lance Corporal brassard. With a sharp glance over to where Sather was kicking the snow, I said, "Got that butt yet?"

"Holy mackerel, you're serious," said Johnson.

"Dead serious. If you don't want to be on a charge do as I say."

Sather looked over at me and when my eye shifted toward him, went back to rooting in the snow. Johnson said, "There, there it is, over there, Joey." And he went over and reached into the snow.

"Alright, since you are both from A Company, I'm gonna let you off with a warning." And with that Lance Corporal Bligh moved off.

Paying an extra dollar for immediate service, I was soon parading my new Lance Corporal stripes, now firmly sewn on each arm on my battledress tunic. Deciding that shoveling snow was beneath a lance corporal, I voted against re-joining the felons, Ralphie and Ears in favour of going to my room. One pace into the room and I realized I was sharing a room with two privates.

"Won't do. Won't do it all" I said to the three beds.

Off I went to petition the Company Quartermaster for a single room that I knew was empty. The CQ was not around, but once I told the stores corporal I was coming from Garrett's office, which was nearly true, he said no problem and congrats–gave me a key and by 1600 hrs, Lance

Corporal Rabbi Hawkins was settled in his new Lance Corporal's quarters.

Some readers might wonder about my minor deviation from the straight and narrow in reference to getting a new room. The astute among you would see that I hadn't lied and that at this time I was not a wholly reformed rabbi. But Rome wasn't built in a day. I would've gotten a single room eventually, all I was doing was sliding a touch of efficiency into the process. I admit it, even a Rabbi can't change his spots overnight.

The next afternoon, just after lunch, Johnny Doyle dropped by. I was in my room reading up on the Queens Regulations & Orders, Vol II, Discipline. Already familiar with it from the point of view of the defence, I now wanted to learn it from that of the prosecutor.

"Lance Corporal Hawkins, your platoon sergeant presents his compliments, would you please go and round up two privates and take them to stores and have them draw cleaning equipment and then proceed to Building D-49, the old barrack block. You're to move all of the beds out of the old platoon room and stack them in the linen storeroom and clean up both rooms."

My good friend, Johnny, message delivered, relaxed against a wall, unaware that he was in the presence of the military version of Jekyll and Hyde added, "Well done, Rab, Probably get 2i/c of a section with it."

My half-crazed officious mode surfaced, and I put down the book and looked sternly at him, "Private

Doyle, we may have been pals in the past. That's over. It's Corporal Hawkins from now on."

Johnny looked around, "No one here but us. No need to play that game."

"Doyle!" I spoke louder, shaking my head, "No game. You will address me as Corporal wherever we are. Doesn't matter if it's smack dab in the middle of downtown Toronto amongst a million people or it's just the two of us in the middle of the Sahara desert. You got it?"

Before Johnny could respond I went on, "And get up to attention when you're speaking to an NCO. You understand me?"

Johnny, dumbstruck, nodded.

"And don't you nod at me, you horrible little shower. It's Corporal."

"Err, yes, Corporal. Got it, yes." Johnny was probably more stunned at my performance than I was. But he recovered quickly and with a look that said drop dead, he gave me both barrels, "Fine, You want Corporal, Corporal it is. Yes, Corporal, no Corporal and three bags full, Corporal. You happy? Then go stuff it in your kit bag, Corporal." He turned and left.

"I didn't dismiss you, Doyle." Johnny never looked back. "That's insubordination, Doyle!"

Johnny ignored me and moved off down the hall. Just in time, I realized that to take it further would result in the platoon and the company laughing at me. I could haul Doyle up in front of the Company Sergeant Major and Garrett would bellow with laughter.

Telling myself I was being magnanimous, but more afraid of the laughter, I let it slide, put on my tunic and balmoral and headed off to round up some peons that I could lord it over in my first command role.

I rounded up Private Rob Crockett, another old pal of mine who was now off limits, at least in my eyes, as well as Private Les Norris. I sent them to company stores to get cleaning equipment and told them to meet me at the building. I arrived before them. The lock was stuck and I had to force the door. Once open I took a walk through it, leaving it hanging off one hinge. Hopefully, there was no regular security check of the place. A temporary building used to house the builders of the camp, it was getting past it's prime. It hadn't been occupied since before I had joined and the heat had been set to just above freezing. I gave the radiators a shot, but they were stuck on their last setting. When the clean up crew arrived with their mops, buckets, brooms and garbage bags, I told Crockett and Norris there was no heat, so if they kept busy they'd stay warm.

Barker and Bobby Marshal arrived as I was exercising my powers as a supervising lance corporal. Both had been good friends of mine and until recently my roommates. I expected to have to come down hard on both of them.

They came into the dusty old barrack block, dripping snow and slush all over the spot where my Staff had already finished. I was way down at the far end and as they saw Crockett sweeping towards them they set out to intercept him. I was busy closely supervising Norris, so all I could do was watch them out of the corner of my eye. "Norris, you missed a place. No, no, go left six inches. There. Very good."

Norris said, "I saw it. I was getting to it."

"No back talk," I straightened up and looked around and spotted Bobby and Barker, now standing with Crockett. I marched over to set them right. "Sorry lads, these men are busy. We can't have interruptions. I suggest you see them later."

Barker spoke softly to Bobby, "Doyle's right. Hawkins has gone off his pumpkin."

"Sounds like a poor copy of Merryfield," answered Bobby in the same low voice. I heard both of them, but I figured they were testing me. I played deaf.

Barker, this time louder, and toward me said, "not here to see them, Lance Corporal, here to see you."

They moved toward me. I held up a hand, "no, stay there, I don't want you messing this place up. They've already cleaned this area… Marshall, you're a walking avalanche, get back outside and kick that snow off your boots. We're cleaning up in here!"

Bobby looked at Barker, who whispered, "do it. We're on a bigger mission. Remember the kids."

Bobby gave me a hard look and left. He went out onto the stoop and using the doorframe to keep balanced, he banged one boot and then the other.

Barker asked me for a donation, but I was only catching a bit of it. I had been busy watching Bobby at the door messing with a balmoral. I heard, "So, what do you say, Lance Corporal?"

"I'm sorry, Private Barker, I am not able to donate to what has historically been a private's endeavour. Now, if the Corporals had such a charity, I'd be pleased to donate."

Barker shrugged, looked a bit disbelieving but I didn't have time for this, "now if that's all," I paused, swept the room with a gesture, "we've got a lot to do."

Barker said, "Yeah, looks pretty important. Probably orders had come down from Ottawa, put Lance Corporal Hawkins on this top secret task. He's the man we need to get an old building swept out. Can't believe how we ever survived without Lance Corporal Hawkins on the scene."

Bobby laid a hand on his friend's arm. "Yes, Lance Corporal, there's one more thing. I heard you say about the privates' and corporals' charities. That's fine, but I must say I don't believe any of this."

Barker shook his head, "I can't figure it. This ain't you, Rabbi. It ain't you. I don't know what you're up to, but all this horseshit you been pulling... gotta be a reason. Shit. Last night you charged two guys from Mortar Platoon. You're crazy."

"Easy, Private Barker, let's not get into insubordination-territory. I'm going to forget I heard that." I shook my head, "we've been friends a long time. You get a free one."

"How about me, Lance Corporal Jerk, I get a free one, too?" asked Bobby.

"Lads, this conversation is over. Now... and this is a direct order. Privates Barker and Marshall, leave this building and return to your duties."

And with that the high and mighty jerk turned back and prepared to lash his galley slaves. A bit later, while I was watching Norris, Crockett came up to me, "Lance Corporal Hawkins,"

"Yes?" I said, thinking that at least some of them recognized my rank.

"I'm going on Christmas leave this afternoon." Crockett grinned at me. I do admit we had been fairly close at one time. He had had me back to his Private

Married Quarter frequently for suppers and barbecues. In the old days, BP, Before Promotion, I'd practically been an uncle to his kids; I'd been a groomsman at his wedding.

"Good, Crockett, leave starts next week for the battalion, how come you're going so early?"

"My wife called me this morning and told me I'd been accepted for a part-time job as a driver for the local brewery."

"Sounds good, a little moonlighting. And the Sarn't Major, he say anything?"

Crockett nodded, "yeah, Garrett went to the OC and they gave me an extra week."

I stared at Crockett, "our Garrett? The maddened Bear gave you an extra week's leave and the OC went for it?"

"Yes, told me it would be classed as compassionate leave and not charged against my annual."

This time I nodded, "well, I'm glad for you, Crockett. But, we're on something extra here. Best to get back to work."

"But that's just it, Rab… I mean Lance Corporal, I can get a trip in early if I report at 1400 hours. That'll get me out of the brewery by 1500 hours and up to Three Rivers by nine this evening and then back first thing."

"What time does your pass say leave starts, Crockett ?"

"Oh, 1600 hours " He was still grinning.

I held out my arms, palms up as if that was final. At the time I felt this was the hard part of the job; making former friends see that the Army doesn't run on friendship, but rather on regulations. I made sure he understood, "Crockett, if the Company Sergeant Major gives you an extra week and it starts at 1600, then I have to abide by that timing."

He looked at me as if I was insane. "You mean you won't let me go early?"

"I'm sorry, Crockett, but if the Company Sergeant Major wanted you to go early, he would have stated that on the leave form. Now, let's get this place finished up. The quicker we get done, the sooner you'll be free to go on your moonlighting job." I shook my head. "Even if it's against all the rules. We are not permitted to hold a civilian position in case we are suddenly deployed."

"Yeah, sure, Lance Corporal. And maybe the Russians will be coming over the pole while we're on Christmas leave." Crockett turned back to his sweeping and I went to see how badly Barker and Bobby had left the front steps. I got there and found my balmoral dripping from its hook just inside the front door. I had wondered why Bobby had taken so long cleaning off his boots. Now I knew. He had filled my balmoral with snow and slush.

The next morning while at breakfast, I overheard the news from a couple of guys from Alpha Company. And while it wasn't complimentary, it sounded accurate.

"Seems some horse's ass Lancejack kept Robbie on too long and he had to take a late shift. If he'd gotten off camp sooner he'd never have had that truck," said the one I knew as Suds Sutherland.

"Yeah, hijack a beer truck. Good idea, I guess," said Chalmers, who I didn't know except by name.

"Better'n doing the job on a spinach truck, eh?"

"Yeah,"

"one of his buddies and he stabs him in the back. Jerk."

"Hey Suds," I said from the table behind them. Sudsy Sutherland turned, a big, skinny guys, all knobs and joints like a human erector set. And no, before you ask he couldn't hit the gym floor with a basketball. He was just tall.

"Hey, Hawkins, heard you got made up. Some kinda company, Delta, eh? Promotes it's most rottenest private."

I held back my natural inclination to climb all over him. Sounded like they were talking about Crockett. And it wasn't good news. Needing to get information out of him, I mentally wrote him up for next time.

"what's this about a beer truck hijacked?"

Chalmers, the other guy said, "hijacked last night up on the highway." He pointed at me. "One of your guys was driving a beer truck." And then they gave me a ping-pong report of the incident.

"Yeah, he's in pretty bad shape."

"Broke his arm."

"Gave him dozens of stitches to his head."

"Kicked him around."

"He's in the hospital."

"Ours?" I asked.

Suds shook his head, "come on, Man, not ours. In Fredericton."

"Yeah, couldn't get someone over at the camp hospital to put a band-aid on you without them getting their fingers stuck."

I said nothing. I stood up and picked up my tray and headed off. I was feeling sick over Crockett but I told myself I had been doing my job. That kind of medication didn't do much for my mental health. I went over to our building and went back to my old room.

As I neared the open door I heard Barker say, "Hawkins, that power-crazed lunatic…"

I stepped into view, then walked into the room. Along with Barker there was Johnny and Bobby. And over in a chair in Bobby's bedspace sat my old Depot buddy, Jeff Allen. Jeff was now a Lance Corporal in A Company. Depot was the term for basic training.

"What did you say, Barker?" I said.

"Wasn't talking to you, Hawkins."

"That's Lance Corporal, to you."

They ignored me. Jeff stood up and came over to stand between me and the private soldiers in the room. I was glad to see that he was going to back another Lance Corporal in a mini-mutiny. He stood in the middle, turned to look at me, then slowly swung around to look at each one of them and said, "Rab, you've disappeared. We've been through a lot, you me and now you're running around like someone shoved QR & O books up your ass. We were in the field for a week a patrol exercise and word trickled down to us that Hawkins had been promoted to Lancejack. I was thrilled." He stopped, shook his head, took a look up at the ceiling. "You have been a natural leader since day one of our days in Depot. Hearing you bein' made up to Lance Corporal, that was terrific news for me. I'm one of your biggest fans."

"Jeff, you mean was?" said Bobby.

Jeff turned. "Bobby, you've been with him since the Recruiting Depot. You've known him the longest, and when we ran into the crap with Geoffrey, you stepped up to say forgive and forget. Remember?"

Bobby nodded, "I remember. An' I remember when I was in kindergarten, too. Both old news. You don't know him now..."

"Hell, his mother wouldn't know him now, Jeff," threw in Barker.

Jeff turned back to me," Hear that Rab? Your fan club is disintegrating. Shit!"

He walked back to his seat, and as he did so, I saw that even with our rank tying us together that Jeff was siding with the mutineers. He sat there, now part of the mutiny that was shaping up. He looked toward Bobby as I said, "Jeff, that was all in the past. It's not part of the equation. We, you and me, we're part of the infrastructure. We uphold the..."

I had pushed him too far. Jeff whirled back to face me, anger boiling out of his pores. "Equation! Infrastructure? Can you hear yourself? Don't' throw that university nonsense at us. I've got grade eight, if you count two years in grade four. I don't know equation. I know people and suddenly you ain't one. Goddammit! You're Rabbi Hawkins, the mad man of the First Battalion. Gotta problem, go see Rabbi. Need help with some barrack room lawyering, go see Hawkins. He's Perry Mason in combat clothes." Jeff went back to head shaking. "And now? Now you're practically slamming people up to a firing squad for walking on the grass. Even as a recruit you felt that every blade of grass in camp had to feel the stamp of Hawkins' boots. The shit you've pulled in this man's

Army, you should be doing thirty years in the crowbar hotel in Valcartier." Jeff ran down.

I felt it was my duty to try and help him out. "Jeff, you've said a lot of things. You're a Lance Corporal, you're entitled..." He started to speak, I waved him to silence. "No, I'm talking. You've had your rant. Now it's my turn. We hold positions of authority within the Battalion. I was wrong to do the things I did, or even encouraged. Well, I've seen the light. I am a reformed Rabbi." I turned back to the wild bunch who had been statues while Jeff and I debated. "As for you lot. I'm sorry if the Army doesn't work the way you want it to. It's still the Army and I am a Lance Corporal in it and the whole damn bunch of you will address me that way. Got it?"

Barker looked at Doyle, at Jeff, at Bobby and then back at me, "no Hawkins. Not in this room, not at this moment."

"What's that supposed to mean?"

Jeff, came out of his chair at a near run, he was so frustrated. He came across the room and poked me on the chest. "It means there's you and there's the four of us. Wanna bet how this is gonna go down if you don't get out of this room now?"

I looked at the faces of my former friends. I saw anger, disappointment and puzzlement. Now Jeff had Judas'd me. There was no discussion happening here and with them all aligned against me, no hope of using my authority. Without another word I left the room. Back in my own room, I stripped out of uniform. I sat on the edge of my bed. Rob Crockett was in bad shape because of me. And I realized I'd lost my friends over the promotion. But what else could I do. I had a job to

Plots in the Pantry

do and friendship didn't enter into it. I undid the tabs on my puttees and unrolled them and then took off my boots, tossed my socks toward my locker and heard the boys head off toward the mess hall, chucking insults at one another. Then, "shush... He's in there."

"What?"

"Hitler Hawkins, that's his new room."

"Yeah, probably reading QR and Os. Hoping to charge somebody."

I looked over onto my bed. Propped open with my bayonet at 118, Conduct to the prejudice of good order and discipline sat a copy of QR and O. I reached over, picked it up and threw it into a corner of my lonely room.

I was mad at myself. I knew I was not acting like Merryfield, far from it. And Merryfield would've been disappointed. "Probably take me out back and kick the shit out of me."

Not aware I'd spoken out loud, I did a little jump as a voice from the hall said, "and it would be deserved, Hawkins, you jerk."

As the footsteps dashed down the stairs, I charged out, but by the time I got to the promenade area, all I saw one flight below was a fire door unconcernedly closing. I slapped the banister and returned to my own room, "he's right, so what would I have done with him? Probably charge the little shit. And proved him even righter."

And so it went. Even after my little confrontation with myself, my reign of terror continued and if anything expanded. Overall, my company was in reasonable shape. Sure they needed a wash and brush up, law and order-wise, but I worked on the worst cases, thinking that I'd get to Delta Company soon enough. But with the remainder of the Battalion in disciplinary disarray, I felt I was needed elsewhere. At first, being a newly promoted Lance Corporal, I didn't leap on sinners from the other companies, but then as I saw how lax their NCOs were I jumped in with both feet.

I didn't realize how deep I had jumped until I was up in the company office picking up some more blank charge reports. I had never realized that upholding the law could be so bureaucratic. Paperwork and more paperwork. From the next office I heard the OC say, "Sarn't Major, you have any occasion to call up Hawkins for any closed-door sessions lately?"

"No, sir. Can't believe that Captain Alfort could have gotten a good idea out of a story book. This works and he'll be a genius. It's early yet, but give the devil his due, from all accounts Hawkins has vanished into the ranks of the regular soldiers. He's been working up at transport with the Transport Sergeant and to all intensive purposes..."

I had tried to stamp it out, I honestly had, but some phrases are butchered and then handed down through the years without any corrections, 'to all intents and purposes' was one of them. I'd heard it in the Depot by corporals, in the Battalion by sergeants and now in the company office by the Company Sergeant Major.

He finished off, "I don't believe it."

"Mmmm, leopards and spots, hey? Calm before the storm, that sort of thing?"

"Bang on Sir. I figure Hawkins is laying low, getting us used to him. Once he's got the ins and outs of the Corporal rank worked out, he'll come out looking to make the big score."

"I heard that, CSM," said a voice that sounded like Captain Alfort. He went on, "good morning, sir. You both discussing our favourite Corporal?"

"Morning, 2i/c, yes, just chatting about Hawkins' absence from Orders Parade. You are to be congratulated for it."

"Yes, Captain Alfort, at this moment you are a genius," said Garrett.

"Two weeks ago I would've been getting ready to say I told you so, that you would regret promoting that son of Satan. And I'm nearly ready to admit it, you have created a miracle,"

"Sarn't Major, I'm glad you said nearly. True, Hawkins is no longer vying against Ralphie Tittleton for most days on CB in a row, but in fact we have invoked the law of unintended consequences."

Garrett said, "a new one on me. But it figures." He paused and then said, "That'd be him. Hawkins breaking a law I've never heard of."

"No, CSM, not Hawkins, us. Me, you and the OC. The law of unintended consequences is something that comes into play when you carefully plan out every detail and then put it into action."

"So how come it's unintended if you meant to do it?"

The OC stepped in, "It's like this, Company Sergeant Major, the consequence is the end result of the action. Here's a classic example of the law of unintended consequences. Right now rabbits are a terrible problem in Australia. Twelve rabbits were brought to Australia and deliberately turned loose around 1860 so that an English country gentleman could hunt them. Ten years later, you could shoot or trap two million rabbits annually without having any effect on the population. It was the fastest spread ever recorded of any mammal anywhere in the world. And all because of a lack of foresight."

Garrett grinned, "So, what you're telling me is that if we're not careful, were gonna have a whole company of Lance Corporal Hawkins types if we don't watch out?"

They all laughed and then the OC said, "So, Fred, what exactly is the unintended consequence of our little brainwave?"

Captain Alfort looked at his boss, "Seems that while we have been free and clear of any shitstorm, the rest of the Battalion has taken it on the chin."

"Oh?"

"Yes, sir. I just came from coffee break at the Mess and it seems that A Company has three, B Company has four, Charlie a whopping seven and Support Company two."

"And those numbers? They represent what, Fred?"

Garrett got it first. "A wild guess says that's the number of times Hawkins has been charged by other Corporals, Sergeants and Warrant Officers?"

"Not quite, CSM. But close. He's the charger, not the chargee. Those figures reflect the number of charges Lance Corporal Hawkins has laid in the last four days."

I had no idea that I had been brought so many criminals to justice. Happy days. But then. as I stood near the wall listening to the three of them, I realized that they were unhappy with my performance. To a degree, so was I. Doing my job was costing me my friends and some level of sanity. I had already alienated the Corporals and Lance Corporals in the Junior Ranks Club by suggesting that they could be doing a whole lot more in the way of cracking down on the privates in the Battalion. Wilbur, being a tad overloaded with Happy Hour beer had even wanted to take me outside and 'beat the livin' crap outa ya, Hawkins'. It didn't get far. Poor old Wilbur struggled to his feet, tripped over a table then fell into a tray of beer. He was shoved under another table and promptly fell asleep. The rest of them settled for calling me names and then forbidding me from sitting at any of their tables.

"But that's sixteen charges..."

I cleared out of the Company office before I heard any more and went off to ponder this latest bit of news.

Things came to a head within the platoon up at the Transport compound where I was overseeing vehicle maintenance. After a quick coffee, I arrived back to find the platoon's armoured personnel carriers deserted. I heard voices coming out of the back of a deuce and a half. Hiding, I thought, remembering a tactic I had employed with great success prior to my promotion. I guess the OC wasn't far wrong when he said, 'takes a thief to catch a thief'. But I was now a reformed Rabbi. The thought occurred to me that maybe it was time to change that name. It belonged to an outlaw. I was now an enforcer. I shunted it to the backside of my brain and stepped around the truck to stand facing the back of it.

"What are you lot doing? You're supposed to be cleaning vehicles not standing around gossiping like washerwoman."

The boys, Les Norris, Barker, Johnny and Bobby were sitting in the back of a deuce and a half sipping coffee. "We're sitting, not standing," came a voice from the dark interior.

"It's coffee break," said Norris.

I shook my head, "Incorrect, lads, the proper term is, it's coffee break, Corporal."

"Yeah, thanks, so it is. Well done, Rab," said Barker.

"Yeah, hey, Rab's a big-shot Lance Corporal, but he still comes around and tells us the time," added Johnny Doyle.

"Knock it off you insubordinate jerks."

"Jerks? Did the big-shot Lance Corporal stoop to calling his subordinates names?"

"Hey, Rab," said Bobby. "I'm sure you've got rules and regulations against that, right?"

"You gonna charge yourself, Lance Corporal?"

I ignored them. Problem was they were right–abuse of inferiors, article 103.28.

"Very well, have your juvenile humor. But... Have it on your own time. It's now 1031, coffee break ended at 1030. Get back to work."

Standing there a few feet from the back of the truck, dressed in kilt and battledress jacket I was angrily slapping my swagger stick against my kilt.

Barker leapt up, came to attention, "his Majesty has spoken. Come on lads, coffee break's over."

And with that, he stepped toward the end of the truck and jumped off. He landed a few feet from me, pretended to stumble and fell against me, knocking my swagger stick out of my hand. As it fell, Barker stamped down on it. He looked up at me. "Oops, looks like I broke the Lance Corporal's little toothpick."

The rest of them laughed.

"That's assault, Barker. I'll have you up on a charge."

"What for, Lance Corporal?" said Bobby as he too jumped off the truck, landing on the stick and breaking it into even smaller pieces. The others followed suit and I was staring down at matchsticks and wood chips.

"That's dumb insolence. You're all on charge."

"Go ahead and charge us, Rabbi old boy," said Johnny, as he swung his hands around to encompass the group. "One against four. And we all saw you hit Barker with your stick and it broke. Whose Garrett gonna believe, his hard-working troops or some jumped up little Hitler in a kilt? Come on lads come, let's get out of here."

And the boys left me standing in the gravel staring at my pulverized swagger stick.

***

Alone in my new room thinking of ways to get the men sorted out it seemed to me that the company I lived and worked in had become complacent, the lads bone idle, dress was slipping. Why I had even spotted Private Walker, the company's sharpest soldier leaving the Junior Ranks Club without wearing his balmoral. And that recent incident at Transport was a perfect example of an Army camp running wild. Garrett was slipping, no two ways about it. And how had I, Lance Corporal Rabbi Hawkins not seen this coming? As I lay on my back, careful not to wrinkle my uniform, I pondered the sad state of affairs that the Canadian army was coming to. A knock came at the door. "Come in... No, hold it, I'll be right there." I remembered just in time that I couldn't just let anyone in, especially not privates. I got up, brushed off my kilt, tugged the battledress tunic into place and went over and opened the door.

There stood Bobby Marshall... Private Marshall, along with Privates Doyle and Barker.

"Yes?"

"Hi, Rab, thought we'd come and try again to get off on the right foot."

"Yeah, you're a Lancejack, and we came to say well done. And to apologize for the swagger stick," said Bobby.

"Thanks, Private Marshall, and you too, Private Doyle. Appreciate that... And I'd appreciate it if you would remember that while we went through Depot together, times change and we cannot live in the past."

"Who's living in the past? Came over to take you to the Mess and buy you a beer."

I shook my head, "Sorry Private Marshall, thank you very much, but I'm afraid it would be unbecoming for me to associate publicly with the men." I started to close the door. Bobby stuck a big sneaker in the way and as the door moved he jammed it with his shoulder.

"Hawkins, this has gone far enough," said Johnny from behind Bobby. "You can't just suddenly stop being Rabbi and start acting like Mollesworth," said Barker. Mollesworth had been our section commander when we had first arrived from Depot, and he was the perfect example of a jackass with Corporal stripes.

"Private Marshall, this is not the proper way to do things. I'll have to insist that you get back from the door and leave me alone."

"C'mon, Bobby, let him alone. Guy's a jerk," said Barker.

"Yeah, sure ain't our Rabbi," added Johnny as Bobby stepped back from the door, "Let's go. He can drink on his own."

"Hold it, Barker and you too, Bobby. We came here for another reason. Not just a beer. For the sake of Crockett's kid... Eh? Whaddya say?"

Bobby, already part way down the hallway said, "Wasta time, Barker. Little Hitler'll just say no."

as we stood there, me in my doorway, the three of them scattered along the corridor, Jeff came up the stairs and walked over to us. "Good afternoon, lads, having a little session with the good Lance Corporal Hawkins?"

Bobby said, "Room, attention! Lance Corporal Allen on deck. Private Bobby Marshall, reporting for duty, Corporal!" Doyle, puzzled started to say something and then got it. He gave Barker an elbow in the ribs and then he too, jumped up to attention. Barker grinned his cheeky grinned and followed suit.

"Knock it off, you clowns," said Jeff. "I'm here to see the Lance Corporal. Maybe go for a beer."

"Yeah, he might drink with you. Just shot us down," said Doyle.

"And we came for a favour," said Bobby. He looked at me, "Same as last year, Lance Corporal?

You'll continue to play Santa for the disabled kids, right?"

"Wrong, wrong oh, wrong oh, Private Marshall." I pulled myself up into a position of attention and said, "can't do it. I'm a Lance Corporal." To emphasize this I swung around to point out the single stripe on my upper arm. "Beneath my dignity. Sorry, lads. Appreciate the thought, but this year it's a no-go."

I waved to Jeff, "why not Lance Corporal Allen. He's a bit chubbier than me. He'll need fewer pillows." I even grinned at them, trying to make it a little joke. Whatever amiability I had tried to inject into the meeting frosted up quicker than a winter's night in Winnipeg.

Jeff's offer to go and have a beer with him glaciered-up as well. "I may be a bit chubbier, but in case you haven't noticed, Hawkins, I'm black. You think the crowd would love a black Santa, hey, Lance Corporal high and mighty?"

I looked at him. Then I looked back at Barker who said, "Forget it, Jeff, Lance Corporal, why not you. You've done it for a couple of years now?"

I almost succumbed. For a minute it felt like my old Rabbi-self was back, but then I shook my head, "Can't do it, Private Barker. Beneath my dignity as a NCO. I'm sorry. Must mean a lot to you, but Bobby's...I mean Private Marshall's much better suited, don't you think? Got that tubby look about him."

"Shit, Rab, he can't do it. You know he's tried. The kids hate him."

"Easy, Barker, they don't hate me. I just get tongue-tied up on that chair." And Bobby came back to the door, "And never mind those fat boy cracks, Hawkins. I'..."

"You're becoming a pain in the ass, Rab," said Jeff. "And I suppose you ain't gonna chuck in twenty bucks for them either, eh?"

I started to close the door. "Sorry, Corporal Allen, not this year. I'm going to be needing my money for new uniforms."

As the door began to close, the boys turned away, Jeff added one more comment, "Bobby was wrong, Rab, you ain't Little Hitler, you're Ebenezer Scrooge."

I'd love to say that this whole mess was solved by the genius that was Rabbi Hawkins. Unfortunately, it was Jeff who gets the credit. Once things returned to normal, or as normal as it gets in a Battalion, I learned from Jeff how he came up with the idea. And to be fair, he did say that he had used Rabbi's Way to get it sorted out. When I asked him what exactly Rabbi's Way was, he said, "You take a problem and grab some plan out of mid-air that you think will solve it. You start with a great idea, beat the shit out of it until anything that's logical or practical or even has the faintest touch of commonsense..."

"And then I build on it, right?"

"Wrong. You trash it. Finally, when you've got a crazy plan that only a lunatic could love, you snatch it and run with it."

"That's not Rabbi's Way, Jeff. That's the way officers think."

"Guess you're gonna be an officer some day, then, Rab." But later, on reflection, I saw that his explanation of Rabbi's Way did have some merit. Even

Pritchard-Ingalls had commented, more than once, on how my plans bordered on...insanity.

And even as I was going down with the ship they didn't quit on me. After it was all over I was grateful, but at the time I found the bunch of them annoying. Jeff and Barker gave it one more try and invited me to go with them to visit Private Crockett in hospital. He was now able to receive visitors and had been moved out of critical condition. Barker stood on his head trying not to lose his cool, even called me Lance Corporal.

But I turned them down flat. "He's a Private. Normally a good leader would have no compunction of visiting his soldiers in hospital, but he's not one of mine. I'd feel like I was trespassing on another section commander's territory, after all, Private Crockett's one of his."

"No compunction? Are you crazy? He's one of your best friends. Trespassing?"

Rabbi nodded calmly, "Lance Corporal Allen, the word refers to..."

"I know what it means."

"Then I shouldn..."

"Means you are a complete moron."

He turned, "We're outta here. We might be trespassing."

I felt sick as I watched them leave. Jeff had saved my life in Depot and Barker had been a friend since we had come to the battalion. On top of that, Jeff was right. Crockett was a very good friend. So was Barker and all Barker had done was give me a glare. Did I turn them down because of the trivial excuse of rank or because I didn't think I could face my buddy knowing that I was responsible for his injuries?

It was sometime after that hospital visit that Jeff had had enough of Lance Corporal

T-yrant, emphasis on 'rant'. Jeff told me that after seeing Rob and his wife, who had been visiting him in hospital, he knew that I needed to come and see, as well as talk, to Crockett and get it settled. He told me that Crockett didn't hold any hard feelings about the beer truck attack.

Much later, Jeff told me that when he thought of the plan, he went looking for someone to tell it to. He found Barker, sound asleep. He yelled and Barker came out of his bed like a claustrophobe in a closet. "What...?"

"Listen. Keep sleeping if you want, but listen." And Jeff outlined his plan. As he talked to a dozy Barker he noticed a postcard on Barker's bedside table. It was for me but the runner had left it in my old room. Jeff recognized the handwriting as being from Beau. Beau was in the Armoured Corps, a tanker, who had been in Depot with Jeff, Bobby and I. He had written that he was coming to spend Christmas with Audra and her parents. That had helped cement the plan in Jeff's head. He stopped telling Barker the plan, went and phoned Beau to see if he and Audra would participate. Beau said of course. Loved the idea. Jeff got back to find Barker had dozed off again. He had to re-tell Barker the plan again because Barker had told him he remembered nothing except a fire drill.

"Wasn't a fire drill. Was me, telling you the plan."

"Tell it again."

And so after first parade, Jeff came over from A Company grabbed Barker and they went off to see Garrett. What follows is the story Jeff gave me on how he put Rabbi's Way into action.

"Nope," said the company clerk, "CSM's in with the OC and 2i/c. Been there a while. Even some loud voices ranting about Rabbi."

Jeff nodded, "see, Time is ripe. Garrett will be ready for this."

"Garrett, Lance Corporal Allen? You dare address me as Garrett in my own Company lines?" came a gruff voice from the hallway. "You forgotten the rank structure since leaving D Company?"

Jeff and Barker spun around, coming to attention as they faced a grim-faced Company Sergeant Major.

"Sorry, sir. Permission to see the Company Sergeant Major, sir?"

"Yeah, yeah" He looked at his watch. "I spend three quarters of my day on Hawkins. May as well spend what's left of it on his buddies. Get in my office." They entered and were told to sit. "Well?"

"Sir, we have an idea that might get Hawkins back to normal."

"Hah. He was never normal. And if it's a firing squad, the Major has already shot that idea down."

"No, sir it goes like this."

When Jeff had finished Garrett said "Are you crazy, Allen?" He shook his head, sipped his coffee, spun his chair around and looked out the window. Jeff told me that it was an issue yellow melmac cup. No sign of the geisha cup and no one mentioned it.

Garrett spun back and pointed his finger, "You are getting just like him." He shifted his finger toward

Barker, "And you've been around long enough to know better." This time Garrett jerked a thumb back toward Allen, "he went through Depot with the son of a bitch. You, Barker, have no excuse."

Jeff told me that he didn't think that this was the right moment to mention that the plan was based on Rabbi's Way. "Okay, gimme the highlights one more time. But hurry it up. We've got an Orders Parade coming up. Yes, Hawkins will be giving evidence. It's one of his." Jeff threw in a little aside about Garrett. "And Rab, I swear. Garrett sighed. Me and Barker heard the Bear sigh." And with that, Jeff got on with his recital.

"You put Rabbi in charge of a TDM guard. The company puts a deuce and a half into the TDM–it will be filled with our props. Even if he checks, he learns nothing." Jeff said that for a long minute there wasn't a sound from the office. Said that he thought Garrett had gone to sleep, so he spoke up, "If it works, we get the old Rabbi back."

Garrett said, "Which is not a plus for me."

Jeff grinned, "True. For you, Sarn't Major, this is probably a lose-lose kind of situation. But it'll cut down on your paperwork and orders parades."

"There's that."

"Anyway, he's got a dozen men in there. He sets up a duty roster and after he goes to bed we sneak in. And we've got Corporal Merryfield in on this…"

Garrett said, "Jake's in on this?"

Jeff answered, "Yes, sir. He thinks it's a great idea."

Barker told me later that that bit was just an adlib from Jeff. At that time they hadn't discussed it

172

with Merryfield. Jeff grinned as he re-told the tale, adding, "I came up with a plan you could only call pure 'Rabbi's Way' shit; do it and then ask for permission." i ignored the comment, "Keep it coming, get the story over with."

"Then Garrett says," Okay, go on. You let him get to sleep and then what?"

"And then we toss in a smoke grenade. Once it explodes, a bunch of us charge in keep him in his bed and gun tape him to the bed. Then out of the smoke comes Jacob Marley–who will actually be Merryfield."

Garrett said, "it's loony." He shook his head, "it's not the least bit convincing." He stared at Jeff and then at Barker, shaking his head, "No, not credible. You…" And the finger came back to point it Jeff's heart. "You actually want to stage a play on Christmas Eve at the Camp Ammo Dump? Put on your own version of the Christmas Carol in hopes it will shock some sense into a lunatic Lancejack. That right?"

"Bang on, Sergeant Major."

Garrett looked at Barker and said, "You help with this plan?"

Barker said, "No, sir, and I agree, it's kinda lame." He shrugged, "But it's all we've got."

There was silence and then Garrett said, "Not lame, lame means unable to walk regular-like. This plan is comatose. If I didn't know better, I'd have said this plan could only have come from Hawkins himself. This has his fingerprints all over it."

"No, sir," said Barker, as he jerked a finger at Jeff, "It's all out of that man's brain."

Garret nodded, "Allen, in Depot did you live in the same room as Hawkins?"

Jeff grinned, he knew what was coming. "Top bunk, right above him."

"Why am I not surprised?" The place turned into a library again; silence.

And furthermore..." Garrett polished, leaned over and pulled open a drawer in his desk. He took out a bottle of scotch and two small glasses. He put the glasses in front of himself. Jeff and Baker turned to stare at each other, then stared back at Garrett.

In another aside, Jeff said, "all I could think of was what the hell was going on in the battalion? We've got a power-crazed Lance Corporal −one who as a private bent every rule he didn't break, suddenly becoming Mr. Law and Order. And our CSM, a man who can trace his ancestry back to Attila the Hun, suddenly offers two of his private soldiers a drink from his private stock."

When Jeff said that I realized I had put Garrett on the edge of desperation.

Garrett poured a full shot into each glass and than twice as much into his coffee cup. As he screwed the top back on the bottle, he gestured with his head, "pick'em up, lads." He put the bottle away and lifted his cup in a toast. Jeff and Barker leaned over Garrett's desk and picked up a glass each then held them up.

"No mix, Sarn't Major?" asked Jeff.

"I've killed men for diluting that Scotch, Allen." He took a large gulp.

Jeff picked up his glass and took a big slug. He said it burned going down, burnt when it got there and burned as it came back up.

"Allen! Not a drop. I warn you. Not a drop!"

Jeff had his hand clasped firmly over his mouth and managed to get it all back down. As Jeff struggled, his eyes screwed shut, Barker grinned, took a little sip and said, "that's not bad, Sarn't Major."

Garrett ripped his eyes off Jeff. "Not bad? You little pipsqueak…"

Barker said, "This tastes like White Horse scotch. I'd say it's been aged 12 years. My tipple is Ben Nevis, a scotch that's 21 years old."

"Oh. Well, Barker, for your information, this is GlenFiddich Solera Reserve and it's 15 years old," said a chastened Garrett, who didn't stay chastened for long. "Hawkins. That man doesn't deserve you two, or Marshall, for that matter."

Barker looked at Jeff who could only nod. Barker turned back to the Sergeant Major, "Sir, Rabbi's a good man. He's a good soldier. He's off the rails a little bit but that's all."

"Off the rails a little bit? He should be de-railed permanently."

He stopped, sipped again and said, "oh hell. Give me the rest of your idiotic story." He looked at Jeff, "come on, Allen, it's scotch, not arsenic."

He reached for Jeff's drink, but Jeff said now he had to finish it off. He pulled the cup back and said, "I'm okay, Sarn't-major."

"Fine. As for the rest of your cockamamie scheme, we need something that makes it credible."

Garrett sipped from his coffee mug. Jeff said, "I'll be able to talk if I were to have a sip of water or coffee."

"Nuts. Swallow and then give. Tell me it's credible."

Jeff said, "that part doesn't matter. Once he's taped to the bed, we drag it out to a central location and stand it up on one end, propped up so he can see everything."

Barker said, "we don't care if he buys it. We'll run it through with him watching. Barker grinned, "And once all the need for secrecy has gone, the rest of the company comes in and sits down in front..."

Garrett said, "tight fit."

Jeff replied, "most of the company'll be on leave by that time. We need to squeeze in maybe forty guys."

Barker chimed in, "And, sir, because you've given him a duty on Christmas Eve, he'll be more like Scrooge than ever."

"I do like it, lads. Sounds too ambitious, too crazy. Too.." He paused, "Too much like something Hawkins would pull. And the time factor? Enough time to get it all together? The script?"

Barker took over the thread, "We think so, Jeff called Lieutenant Audra Shannelly, from the hospital. She's the girlfriend of another of our Depot squad. She'll type out a script based on what Beau, Jeff and a few of the others know about Rabbi, even stuff from his high school teacher from Toronto, a Mrs. Comeau. Seems Corporal Merryfield had her as his teacher as well..." He paused to grin even wider, "According to Depot rumour, she's about five feet nothing and she gave Corporal Merryfield the strap."

The thought of the six-foot-two, armour-plated Merryfield being punished by a little teacher even had Garrett grinning.

My involvement in my own redemption came without an inkling of the devious plot the Company had hatched under the guise of a simple duty. It began with a command performance in front of his Bearness.

"Stand at ease, stand easy." Garrett looked at me standing in front of his desk.

Garrett flipped idly through some papers, looking like he was holding an argument inside his head then coming to a decision, "Lance Corporal, I'm going to have to cancel or at least delay your leave."

"Sir?"

"I noticed you hadn't put in a destination for leave so I assumed that you were staying in camp for Christmas?"

"Well, sir..." That had been my plan until I gotten promoted. Now I was planning to hitchhike home, show off my new rank.

"So," Garrett ignored me. "I have an urgent request for a picket in the TDM. Seems the military police have a deuce and a half full of some kind of secret shit and Staff Sergeant Prichard-Ingalls asked me to provide a guard–ten men and Lance Corporal."

Garrett paused, took a large gulp of his coffee and waited. I knew he was waiting for the raft of excuses I would shovel toward him at the mention of work, but this wasn't the Rabbi of yesteryear he was staring at, this was a keen, power-hungry, newly-promoted Lance Corporal. I still think the rapid response shocked him. "Very good, sir. No problem."

Garrett coughed and choke but managed to get his head down and splattered his paper and desk.

"Careful, sir, you're drinking too fast."

He recovered, swallowed, and then began wiping his papers with a boot rag from his shoe-shining drawer. "Yeah, choking while on duty." He looked up at Rabbi, "gotta charge for that, have we?"

"Pardon, sir? Oh... A joke." But neither of us really thought so. Garrett gave me a list of names. I didn't really pay attention to that list. Jeff had given it to him and it contained all my former buddies who volunteered to get me back to being good ol' Rabbi again.

"A truck will pick you all up at 1800 hours on the 23rd. You'll be relieved on the 25th at 0800.

"On Christmas Day, sir?"

"Roger. No further questions, dismissed."

Two trucks arrived at the barracks, the drivers two of Staff Sergeant Pritchard-Ingalls Corporals, got out and explained that I had to supply the drivers from here on to the TDM.

Barker and Doyle volunteered. No one else did, because aside from me, the entire group was in on the plan. Barker took the empty truck, watched the lads toss their rucksacks into the back and climb in. Doyle took the second truck along with a word of warning from one of the Military Police Corporals, "careful with this vehicle, lads, lots of dangerous cargo."

I checked my men, gave and received a thumbs-up from Doyle perched up behind the wheel of the second deuce, then climbed in the passenger side of the first truck and told Barker to head for the TDM.

Upon arrival, I jumped out and opened up the main gate and once the second truck had moved through, closed and re-locked it. We were in the administration area of the TDM. Further in, there was another fenced compound which was guarded twenty-four and seven by a sergeant, a corporal and twenty soldiers. Each unit in the brigade took turns at this. By coincidence, the MacCammons had the duty and two platoons from Alpha Company were manning the barricades on this night.

I got my troops unloaded and moved into the old warehouse. What I didn't know at the time was that Jeff had managed to persuade a group of my former pals to assist in putting twelve beds at the far end and one bed in an old office. Jeff had been there for hours before we arrived. He had stuck a piece of paper on the door that read–Corporal's quarters–thinking that would impress me. It did. I was so impressed me that it fooled me completely. If I had been more alert I would have seen Jeff's little car parked around behind the building. He not being a member of Delta anymore, there was no reason for him to even be here.

I wasted no time reading the riot act to my men, expecting a load of bitching, but they were all in the plan and all I saw was a strangely enthusiastic bunch of press-ganged soldiers forced to work on Christmas Eve. With them sworn to both cooperation and silence no matter what crazy orders I issued, they were obeyed. Give me credit, I had made up a watch list of two people on for one hour at a time. By the time everything was ready, it was 1930.

I set the first two guards in place near the trucks, saying, "stay at least three yards away at all times. We're guarding dangerous cargo. No one is to go near the vehicle or poke around in the back. Any questions?" There were none. I left to go back and harass the remainder of my crew.

To put this in proper perspective you need to understand the sequence of events. For a lot of it I wasn't present. I got a big de brief from the boys a couple of days after Christmas. By then I had relinquished my single room and had moved back in with Barker and Bobby. It was in that room, as we finished off the last of the beer that they all tossed in their two cents. There was Jeff, now the only Lance Corporal in the group, Johnny, Barker, Bobby, Vince Kennedy from our Company and stuck in one corner, hogging a couple of quarts of beer, my old pal, Ralphie Tittleton.

Johnny started off by taking the story from after I had left the first shift, and gone back into the building. He had waited until I had gone back inside our Staff building and closed the door. He then snuck over to the back of the truck. It had been parked with its nose toward the front gate. Morgan, the second sentry went over to the other gate and met up with Prichard-Ingalls, Major Charles, Captain Alfort and Sergeant Major Garrett. He gave them an update and they all trooped back to update the rest of Delta Company. They had been stashed in another empty building earlier in the day by Garrett. When I look back on it, I remembered that our quarters had been deserted but at the time I hadn't paid any attention.

Amazingly enough, my duty bunch settled in quickly and quietly, giving me no reason to lay a charge on any of them. Around 2330 I told them that if there was any disturbance to waste no time in arousing me. "I don't care if it's a raccoon climbing the outer fence, you make sure to get me up. We'll investigate and then if it's nothing, we can stand back down. But, and you can quote me, 'It's Christmas Eve, all that's going to happen is we all get a quiet night's sleep without any racket or disturbance."

This next bit was told to me by Jeff. "At midnight, I left the building to tell the hidden group that you was asleep. The OC said, "next shift change?"

"Zero-one, Sir."

"How much time do you need?"

"We can set the snatch group up right away, beside the bed. If it looks like he's gonna wake, we'll jump him."

"And then it starts," added Garrett.

"Yes, be nice if we can set up without him waking. But if not, we'll go with what we've got."

"Okay. Let's do it," said the OC.

Jeff went back checked that I was still asleep. Then he went back out and with a few whispers and quite a few shakes of soldiers, got them up and then things started happening. One thing in their favour in which no one had thought of was the backdoor. It was a set of double-doors, both opening wide enough to let two soldiers carry a set of bunk beds out while other soldiers were quietly bringing in two chairs each. There was a tense moment when the entire operation shutdown. Near the exit, Morgan tripped and dropped his end of the bed onto Stiles, who fell onto a pair of chairs. Jeff, standing watch on me in my little room, gathered his assault team and had them prepared to jump on me if I woke up. I rolled over, Jeff whispered, "ready…"

Then I fell back into my steady, low snore. Jeff and his gang relaxed, waited two minutes, then gave the signal for everyone to carry on.

No more problems occurred and finally, around 0230 the scene was set.

Delta Company's main body had successfully transformed a twenty man dormitory into a theatre, complete with folding chairs, a stage and footlights; forty bedside lamps from bedding stores all connected to a number of extension cords.

Jeff told the OC and Garrett all was ready. They took their seats in front and centre and the Major gave Jeff a nod. The game was on. From the audience came excited whispers, shushes and then Garrett quietly stood up, turned and faced the troops and the place went quieter than a graveyard at midnight on Halloween.

Jeff looked around and saw that his key players were in position, the audience were ready and then he pointed a flashlight outside through a back window waved it up and down turned it on and off three times and waited. Seconds later Barker kicked the show off by exploding a thunderflash outside the building near my room. At the same time, a green smoke grenade popped at the other end of the building and as the smoke swiftly spread into the blanketed shrouded bed space, Bobby said my face appeared, shock its main ingredient.

From my point of view, I came awake at the sound of hell igniting. Suddenly monsters from a nightmare fell on me, but I was sure I was awake. I didn't even get upright when the jump team covered me with blankets and then leapt on me, smothering all body movement. The tape team scrambled from the wings and began to tape me to my bed. By this time I was busy screaming orders and yelling threats from deep within the pile. Then ever so slowly, me and my bed emerged into the main room. They placed it gently in the back area of the stage, my head in toward the crowd and the main stage.

They told me that when the main lights went out, the footlights shone out onto the scene and the crowd went berserk, even Garrett was roaring and clapping. It was a clean, well- performed first act and the play hadn't even started yet.

Throughout the company, I had been very well-liked and the sudden transformation into the commandant of Dachau had startled them and angered them. Human nature as it was, they were all thrilled to see Herr Hawkins get his dandies. Once the jump team were done they formed pairs and with a blanket between each pair began to flail the air, clearing away the thick green smoke. Another thunder flash exploded outside, this one with a little twist.

Barker, their one-man demolition team, had noticed an empty garbage can near his site. He tossed the second thunder flash into it and put the lid on, then he shifted quickly out of the way as the big firecracker exploded. Overkill. The lid came off like a moon rocket, rapidly rose four feet and then just as rapidly veered straight at an astonished Barker who ducked as the lid, crashed through the window and came to rest at Jeff's feet. He didn't miss a beat.

I could see people up behind the row of bedside table lamps which had been placed a foot apart and all pointing at the stage; footlights for an improvised theatre. I was stuck up on my bed in such a way as to see both the audience and the players on stage as they came and went. Props were at a minimum. Costumes were even worse. I found out later that the Camp theatre had put on Gidget Goes Hawaiian: The Play, and so Jeff had borrowed the costumes. The first two people came out dressed in beach gear, shorts, T-shirts and cut-offs, clam digger pants, also known as pedal-pushers, and Hawaiian shirts.

Once my gravity had dragged me down the mattress and bed frame so that my feet could stand on the bed end I wasn't too uncomfortable. I couldn't say the same about my emotional state. I was pissed off at Jeff, at Bobby and especially at Garrett and the OC. They were out there laughing as a Lance Corporal in their battalion was being humiliated.

While I hung there, fuming and feeling like I've been crucified with gun tape the show got underway. All the lights, including the main building ones flashed off, on, off stayed off for a good thirty seconds and then only the flood lights came back on.

On centre stage stood a kid's school desk, beaten up, cracked and looking old enough to have been Garrett's grade three desk. Squashed into it and dressed in a bright yellow Hawaiian shirt and pale blue clam diggers was Beau. I used to wear clam diggers at basketball practice and on the trampoline at high school. He was barefoot and had on a straw hat that had been worn by one of the original Israelites who built the pyramids. He grinned over at me then gave a little wave off to the corner. My eyes followed his wave. Beau as a surprise wasn't enough. He was my best friend. Some people say they'd take a bullet for a buddy. Beau had taken a real one for me in basic training. He was now a full-fledged tank driver in the Armoured Corps, stationed in Calgary. Him being here was amazing. But the person he was waving at was obviously the reason for his presence. It was Audra Shannelly, his girl and a Lieutenant Nursing Sister at her camp hospital. They had met when he was recuperating from being shot by a maniac with an SMG. Of course, in my opinion, it was a case of an unarmed maniac charging an armed maniac. Not that I'm complaining. Without that mad dash of Beau's, I wouldn't be here today.

Beau Cratchit made his theatrical debut, "it's freezin' in here."

The crowd, sweat pouring off them, laughed. Then from my room walked Bobby Marshall. "Shut up, Cratchit, if you'd chopped more wood, we'd have a bigger fire, now get back to work."

I started to figure out what they were doing but at that moment I was too mad to see clearly. And Bobby, he was playing me–but a me playing Scrooge. Jeff's comment, "Scrooge Hawkins." rushed up to meet me. There was no doubt Bobby was me. He was wearing my Toronto Maple Leaf sweater number 18; Carl Brewer, and he was stretching the hell out of it. Over top of the sweater and pinned on each arm was a Lance Corporal's brassard. It was a real Toronto Maple Leafs' sweater. One that Brewer had worn in the 1962 season: where the Leafs won the Stanley cup. My father had gotten it for me, telling me that Davey Keon gave it to him for me. Keon and my father were members in the same men's club in Toronto. He said he had been telling Davey about how his son when in high school had worn hockey gloves with the palms cut out like his favourite Leaf, Carl Brewer. Davey laughed and said, "Brewer is our favourite too, but he is a loose cannon."

"Yeah, that's Donnie, as well."

Bobby's wearing of my favourite sweater did nothing to calm me down. But taped and gagged I could only promise myself that he would receive a suitable reward later.

Out from my room, which they were obviously using as the dressing room, came Barker and Johnny in bathing suits. Barker was carrying a surfboard. Johnny was wearing a towel around his shoulders.

Bobby, looked at the crowd and said in a puzzled tone, "All right. Here they are the two portly gentleman as described as by Dickens. But how come they're on before Fred?"

I didn't catch it. I knew they were doing their version of a Christmas Carol, but I didn't know the story line as well as the rest of Delta Company.

Jeff said, "Fred's busy. He'll be along shortly."

Barker shifted the surfboard, which was bigger than him, from one hand to another and then dropped it.

The crowd roared and one witty voice yelled out, "hey, Portly Gentleman Number One, get a grip."

Barker, forgetting himself yelled back, "shut it, Wilbur. The bloody thing's heavy."

Jeff got the story back on track, "Merry Christmas, Rabbi Scrooge, would you care to make a donation to the Homeless Surfers of Oromocto?"

Scrooge Bobby said, "Bah. Humbug. Get out of here or I'll call the military police."

A voice from out of my room yelled out, "hi, Uncle Rabbi Scrooge, sorry I'm late." And out came our Company Second-in-command, Captain Fred Alfort, dressed in a pair of pink shorts, a private soldier's combat shirt and a pair of sunglasses. He looked around at the crowd, then at me, pointed a finger at me, "Hey, looks like you're all tied up."

"What's new, Freddie?" said Bobby. "You're always late. I've never met a nephew like you in my life. Always coming up with all kinds of weird ideas and plans."

The crowd loved it. I heard the OC, Major Jason Charles yell, "typecasting, hey, Fred?"

The news of Captain Alfort suggestion to promote me based on a book he'd read, had flashed through the company faster than a soldier leaving camp on payday.

"Uncle Rabbi Scrooge, I'd like to invite you to Christmas dinner."

"Bah! Humbug! I've got to get home. Besides, you're a private. I don't eat with privates. Beneath my dignity as a Lance Corporal banker and financial wizard. Go on, beat it."

There was another eruption of laughter. I had made a similar statement often enough lately, so often that it was becoming monotonous. Guilt crept up on me, I shoved it away. I was a Lance Corporal. And Lance Corporal's didn't eat with privates. Oh, sure, Corporal Wilbur did, but he didn't do his job. Or did he? I'd never heard of Wilbur charging anyone, yet his section consistently came out near the top in the Battalion's skill at arms competitions, even winning it two years in a row.

As Bobby said, "Beat it." the lights went out and the crowd applauded. The lights stayed out. The place went quiet, disturbed only by some low chatter from the cheap seats, which in this case was all of them.

Sounds of furniture being shifted and then right beside me came Jeff's voice from out of the dark, "due to time constraints, we move on towards Scrooge safe in his house. He's seen and spoken to the face in the doorknob that had been the face of Jacob Marley, his deceased business partner. And Rabbi Scrooge has had his gruel, but it was foul so he didn't eat much of it. He's getting ready for bed when..."

The lights flickered on and off and then with a pause came on and stayed on. There stood Bobby in a nightshirt and wearing my Leaf shirt over it. On his feet he wore combat boots. Offstage came the clink and clank of heavy vehicle chains. And out of the shadows came... One guess. With a Jacob in the play, why not use a real Jacob. Yep, my old Depot nemesis, Lance Corporal, now a full Corporal, Jacob Merryfield, a.k.a., Jake. Merryfield shuffled his way over to stand in front of Bobby. He was wearing his judo pyjama suit, complete with black belt, which he had earned belt by belt, colour by colour. Pinned to each of his sleeves was a full Corporal brassard–two hooks. Draped across his shoulders was a length of links of vehicle tow chain. In one hand he carried a square box that came from the Hinky-Dinky, a fast food dive frequented by most of the camp's living-in-soldiers. He said in his parade square voice, "anybody here order a pizza?"

Bobby reached for it and said, "yeah, me, thanks Jake."

Then, shocked at what he'd said, Bobby immediately jumped back from Jake. Merryfield had been our Lance Corporal, Beau, Jeff, Johnny and me in Depot. For the first eight weeks of training, Bobby was so terrified of Merryfield he couldn't speak his name without stuttering and now he had just realized that he had called Merrifield by his first name. You have to hand it to him though, he recovered fast. Bobby looked around at the crowd and I saw him grin, "okay to call you Jake?"

"Only that once," came Merryfield's voice of doom.

The shocks and surprises kept coming. Talk about your nemesis. Who in the hell, except me, ever got two of them? From somewhere in the crowd came the voice of Nemesis Number Two, military police Staff Sergeant Pritchard-Ingalls, whose voice boomed out, "hey, Jake, you're supposed to be acting."

The crowd went wild and then as they settled down Bobby reached for the pizza again. Merryfield slapped his hand, "no." With his free hand he reached up and pointed at his two books, "this pizza's only for full corporals. It's beneath my dignity to eat with Lance Corporal's."

Boy, oh boy, was I getting it this evening. And did I deserve it? Hardly. I had been the hardest-working corporal or lance corporal in the battalion. Hadn't I charged more privates for more offenses than all of them combined? And hadn't I brought a new wave of discipline and department tsunami-ing across the battalion? And for what? For this. It just wasn't fair. But, I was in the Army because life wasn't fair. I decided I would just ignore this farce.

As he said that, Merryfield opened the box and took out a slice of pizza, took a huge bite out of it and as he chewed said around the pizza, "you, Rabbi Scrooge, you're gonna get three visits from three spirits."

"What do you mean?"

Merryfield swallowed and said, "Whatta you? An idiot? three ghosts are coming for you."

"Oh." Bobby stepped back. "Any suggestions, Jake?"

"Yeah, Scrooge, I've got two. Number one, brace yourself for the visits. They won't be pretty." Merryfield looked over at the crowd with a faint grin on his face. Then I realized that this little bit had not been scripted.

Bobby, as confused as the rest of us, asked, "and number two?"

"Quit calling me Jake."

"Oh. Right, of course Corporal. I mean…"

Merrifield handed Bobby the pizza box to shut him up, then turned to leave. He spun back to stare straight into my eyes and shook his head slowly, "and you. I expected better. Did I waste my time on you?" He gave his chains a rattle and left. That stung. Merryfield had been a contradiction in combat clothing. Tough, fair, but surprisingly considerate when it came to looking after his troops. He could browbeat, wade through their kit and push them to the limit, but let some other Lance Corporal insult us and he faced the wrath of Merryfield.

The lights went out, then Jeff was back beside me with a penlight flashlights which he shone in my face.

I shut my eyes and tried yelling through my gag. Then Jeff pulled it out and said, "we getting through to you?"

"Allen, you're already facing three years less a day. When I get…"

Jeff shoved the gag back into my mouth and said so the room could hear, "no soap, boys. The Supreme Lance Corporal has just charged me with treason and the rest of you with a conspiracy to make a human being out of a law book. Maybe act two will work."

He moved away and the light bobbed off towards my room and then went out.

When the lights came back on, there stood Ghost number one, Johnny Doyle, wearing a bedsheets as a toga, a sombrero and carrying a scroll. He marched up to a silent Bobby who was standing mid-stage with a hand in the pizza box and said, "I am the ghost of Christmas Past."

Bobby, pulled out a slice of pizza, stuffed half of it into his mouth and around that said, "I know who you are. What's up?"

"You. And your past." Johnny unrolled the scroll and began to read from it. "There's no Fizzywig in your life, Rabbi Scrooge. But according to Mrs. Comeau..."

The mention of her name made me think that Merryfield had been in touch with her. She had been his teacher long before she was the vice-principal of my high school. She had actually steered me to Merryfield and the First battalion.

"She tells us you had a good time at high school. You were expelled three times, had eighty-five detentions and at a guess played hooky for a combined total of three months over your four years at high school."

"Hey, Rabbi, your high school career sounds like Ralphie's army one," came a voice from the audience.

Johnny looked up from his scroll, "can it, you lot. Any further outbursts and I'll get Lance Corporal Hawkins out of his bed. He'll settle you down. Course, he's tied up at the moment but…" Judas returned to his scroll, "the next visitor couldn't make it in person, not being a ghost like me, but she did send us her best wishes and hopes that the remedy doesn't kill the patient…"

The lights went out and when they came back on, there was Audra standing beside Barker, facing Bobby and wearing an Oromocto High School cheerleader's outfit? She stood there and started reading from a piece of paper she had in her hand, "dear Donny, I'm sorry to hear that you've become a tyrant. I was thrilled when your mom told me you'd been promoted. Do you still have that Marshall's baton I gave you?"

They were really stooping low. Now they'd recruited my former girlfriend, Judy. She had seen no future with a soldier and we had split up. We were still friends but we weren't keeping in contact much.

"When Jeff called me and told me about your attitude change… the Jekyll and Hawkins syndrome he called it. He's very funny, but he sounds like a true friend."

Yeah, he's priceless. Jekyll Hawkins. He's not funny.

Audra paused and then looking at us said, "it took me a dozen tries to read this without crying. I may not make it this time."

Then my ears, mutinying against me as well, heard Company Sergeant Major Garrett say in a soft and gentle voice, "you'll be fine, Sister. Aside from Scrooge, we're all friends here."

Audra's rank was that of Lieutenant, Nursing Sister. All the nurses in the military were called sister. Audra flashed her heavy-duty smile at us all. I felt my anger cooling. I began to feel guilt, compassion even an appreciation of what these folks were all doing for me. Here was Judy and Audra: two girls who had never met but who both were able to work some kind of magic in me. Hell, not just in me. Audra was in the act of turning that old grizzly bear, Sergeant Major Garrett in to Winnie the Pooh. She looked out at the crowd once more and then back to Judy's letter, "Donnie, you were the only boy in my life since grade seven. Somewhere deep inside me I think I'll love you forever. I fell in love with you the day we moved on to your street. You rode over on your bike and helped my father unload the suitcases from our car. Yes, I'm still in love with you. It's just that I know I can't share you with the Army. Or anyone or anything else. So, while you and I are no longer one, don't let your other love…" Audra burst out sobbing.

We all waited. I had nothing else to do anyway. And I ignored the tears in my eyes created by that damn smoke grenade.

The crowd sat in silence. Soldiers are such sissies, aren't they? Yeah, all of us, me too.

Bobby walked over to Audra, handed her a huge white Army-issue hanky and said, "never been used, Sister."

Audra looked up at him, smiled as if Bobby had just given her the keys to the city and said, "thanks, Bobby."

After she had regained her composure Audra said, "I think Judy has made her point, don't you?"

"No, give him both barrels, Audra," yelled Beau, my bloodthirsty, Armoured Corps faithful companion.

She ignored Beau and looked into the crowd, "anyone else want me to carry on?"

My gag wouldn't let me say no so I just hung there.

Jeff said, "hey, Sister, sometimes the patient needs to take all of his nasty-tasting medicine at once."

Audra smiled, bewitching the entire company, "ouch. Not only do I have a treadhead ordering me around..."

Beau, her boyfriend, was a treadhead, an Armoured Corps wretch.

"But now I've got an infanteer playing doctor."

The gang laughed and Audra went on, "sorry Beau and Jeff, one of you is far too bossy and the other is practicing medicine without a license. Besides, I outrank you both." She folded the letter and held it down by her side as she turned to Johnny and said, "ghost of Christmas Past, move it along."

Doyle stood there. He looked like a startled fawn. There was silence and then Bobby walked over and put a hand on Johnny's arm and said, "so beat it, already, Baby Ghost." He raised one hand above his head and circled one finger in the air. "Lights off, boys, this one's over."

The lights went out. Once again we saw nothing. I heard footsteps scurrying around and the scraping of furniture being moved. When the lights came on there stood Bobby in one corner of a bare stage. In the middle stood Beau, still dressed as Bob Cratchit with Audra in a one piece red bathing suit, the kind that had a frilly dress attached. In between them but a couple of paces further back towards the rear of the stage and dressed in a baseball uniform that was too small for him stood our company clerk, Mouse Clark. The big lump said loudly, "God bless us everyone." He repeated it again, again and again like some kind of mantra, "God bless us everyone." He had started loud to get our attention and then tapered off to a low background mumble.

The usual lights on, lights off routine played itself out and then with the lights on from out of stage left walked or possibly trotted the ghost of Christmas Present. I would've bet money, real money, that nothing could have induced him to come on stage dressed as he was. But there he was; shocking me and everyone else. I think this was the one chunk of the evening where something turned inside my head. Pritchard-Ingalls was dignity enshrined in an Army uniform. Gleaming shoes, creases where they should be and none where they shouldn't. To see him voluntarily put himself on public display in a ridiculous outfit for me came as a jolt. From there it was a simple step to really see the entire façade I had been lugging around with me in my phoney-baloney Lance Corporal masquerade. They hadn't finished with me. Mind you, I wasn't totally reformed when Pritchard-Ingalls did his bit. I was wavering, but I still held onto to the idea that Rabbi was right.

Pritchard-Ingalls was dressed in a horse costume, if a horse ever pranced in on its hind legs. There was his human head but under one arm he was carrying a horse's head. The horse stopped beside Bobby, looked over at me and said, "if that letter didn't melt your heart and open your eyes, then I sure as shit hope my get-up moves you, Hotshot… Scrooge." Staff Sergeant Pritchard-Ingalls had made his entrance.

The combination of Mouse Clark babbling "God bless us everyone." and Pritchard-Ingalls as a horse was too much. The Company was in stitches. My jaws were aching from trying to laugh through a gag. I was laughing so hard my bed shifted. It and me fell over face-first. I hung there, the tape keeping me three or four inches from the floor while both the head and foot of the bed kept me from becoming part of the floor.

Everyone was laughing so hard nothing else happened. I hung there while eighty-plus fools laughed at me. Finally Prichard-Ingalls and Mouse came over and stood me up. Mouse still going on about God blessing us, everyone. Prichard- Ingalls' face was inches from mine, "Hotshot, you do amuse me."

Finally the light crew regained their sanity and the lights went out. Back on, they lit up a new scene. There was Captain Alfort standing beside a girl I'd never seen before. She was in a pioneer style long gingham dress and bonnet and was standing with her back to the audience. A few paces from them stood Prichard-Ingalls and Bobby both not even trying to stifle their chuckles. Bobby said through his giggles, "oh, Ghost of Christmas Present, what is this?"

Prichard- Ingalls started laughing again, "this, Rabbi Hotshot Scrooge, is your nephew, Freddie. We are at his house. And beside him is…" He held out a tree-trunk arm and a hoofed hand toward the couple and said, "His gorgeous wife, Augustine."

As he spoke, the girl turned slowly toward the audience. As the bonnet came around so that we could see who it was, Jeff's black face came into view. Before the crowd erupted again, Jeff yelled out, "Hawkins! You are a jerk! You see the hell you put me through?"

And once again my feelings got the better of me. My eyes started to fill as I saw how far my friends were willing to go to come to my aid. They were right and I was so very wrong. I didn't deserve them. Even Garrett, who I had always assumed was waiting for me to end up on the wrong end of a firing squad that he commanded, in his own way showed some concern over the wretch I had become. Of course, in his case, there was the unstated reason that I was more trouble to him as a Lance Corporal than as a private. But...how true was that?

I missed Jeff's next lines due to self-pity, came to in time to hear Captain Alfort say, "You must understand, my dear, Uncle Rabbi, I mean Uncle Scrooge is a decent Lance Corporal. He's just had a touch too much power."

Jeff swung around to face him. "Touch too much power? That's like saying the ocean is a bit salty. The man's a maniac. Take me home, immediately!"

"Now, dear..." started Captain Alfort.

Jeff swung a black fist up toward the 2i/c's chest, "Don't now dear me. I want out of this insanity!"

Over the laughter, Pritchard-Ingalls' voice rang out, "Hotshot, I may be a horse, but you need to quit being a horse's ass." He waved both arms, "lights! Lights for God sake. Get them out. Put me and Allen out of our misery."

The lights went out.

I stood or rather, hung on the bed frame. The dark hid not only the police horse and Jeff in his dress, but my tears as well. It was a good thing I had been gagged or else they'd have heard me back in camp. It just flooded through me. of course, Judy's letter and Audra's reading of it didn't help. For the past few weeks I'd been some kind of over-the-top, nickel-plated tyrant. I think it was Lord Acton who said that power corrupts and also that absolute power corrupts absolutely. And then there was the saying that a little knowledge is dangerous. I had had both, the absolute power and the clear lack of knowledge. Sure, I could recite by article pretty much all of QR and O, but I didn't know people as well as I thought. I was sobbing, muttering through my gag and wishing I was a million miles away. I was stuck. I wasn't a Lance Corporal and I sure as hell wasn't a private. So who was I now? Who could I be? What would I do when this was over and I had to face my friends? I ran down, hung there, a sad fish in a seafood shop window, eyes glazed. Lost.

The flashlight came back on and loud enough to be heard over the mutterings of the crowd, Jeff said "You ready to come down now, Rabbi?"

I nodded and he removed the gag. Once my mouth was free, I didn't even recognize that it was me speaking." First of all, Jeff Allen, thank you, very much."

In the dim light I saw that Audra had moved up beside Jeff. "Rabbi, it's okay. You're back and you're among friends." Then Beau was there nodding. He said softly, "Yeah, friends."

Audra said, "I'd say we have just experienced the redemption of Rabbi Hawkins."

Once they cut me down off the bed frame, I stood there looking around at all the people who had done so much tonight to make me realize that they were truly my friends. I moved stiffly, a robot suddenly given life. At centre stage, I picked up the garbage can lid and a shoe left by one of the actors and banged it on the lid. When things had quieted down I said, "I'd like to thank you all for taking the time and trouble on my behalf... It's pretty hard to say I'm sorry when in a very real sense I was trying to do a good job. Until tonight I didn't realize that to do a really good job it not only requires the knowledge of how to do that job but it also requires an understanding of people and how to deal with them based on each person's personality and ability. Initially I was proud of my dedication to the job. I don't believe I ever charged anyone who was not guilty." I paused and then went on, "Not like some of the charges I faced as an innocent soldier." And at that, I felt myself grin and the crowd laughed with more disbelief than humor.

Then I heard Garrett say, "The SOB's always been guilty."

And then Pritchard-Ingalls added, "Hawkins, you don't have an innocent bone in your body."

I ignored them both and the catcalls as well as the jeers. "During my recent tenure as a Lance Corporal, I forgot the most important thing a leader must remember; his humanity. Dealing with people means seeing them as people, as different and the same as a bagful of smarties. All different in color yet all containing the same chocolate centre."

"Kinda like me, Rab?" yelled Jeff.

"No, Jeff, not like you," yelled Barker. "Smarties are smart."

Once the hecklers had been quieted by the crowd I said, "tonight I realized that no matter how dopey you act, there is always someone somewhere who'll forget that you are an idiot. I'm fortunate to have not just a someone but a whole rifle company full of someone's, along with a Treadhead, a Nursing Sister and a military policeman."

I felt my cheeks grow warm again and decided to get it done. "This is the best Christmas present I could ever receive. Thank you all. Thank you all."

***

A while later, when everything had returned to normal and yes, I was a Private again, I met Corporal Mouse Clark in the meal line up. He said, "Heard a good one today, Rab. From the Company Sergeant Major. The OC came in to the company office for a coffee and Garrett was there. Garrett said, "It's good to see Hawkins is back to being his usual self, eh, Sir?" The OC said, "What's he doing now, Sarn't Major?" Mouse laughed as he finished his story, "Thirty days."

The End

A Note from the Author: *Many thanks to all who purchased a copy of Plots in the Pantry. Curious as to what happened to Rabbi's buddy in the hospital? Did Rabbi and his pals settle in for a lobster feast? What became of the hijacked beer? Important questions and all answered in the full-length version of "Screwge: The Redemption of Rabbi Hawkins" available online – and for free.*

Recipe for Beer Steamed Lobster Tails

Beer Steamed lobster tails are wonderful when you add plenty of melted butter mixed with lemon juice and crushed garlic.

Prep Time: 7 Min
Cook Time: 8 Min
Ready In: 15 Min
Servings: 2 servings

Ingredients
2 whole lobster tails
6 ounces, approx ½ a can
of beer

Basically add 6 ounces per every two lobster tails. In Rabbi's story they went on to cook 100 lobsters and used a gallon of beer.

Directions
In a medium saucepan, over medium to high heat, bring the beer to a boil. If lobster tails are still in the shell, split the shell lengthwise first.

Place a steamer basket on top of the saucepan.
If frozen, thaw lobsters first. Place lobster tails in basket and cover.

Reduce heat and simmer for 8 minutes.

Depending on the quantity of lobsters, add steaming time by a few minutes per basket of lobsters. Add more beer if there is the danger of the container boiling dry.

Author Contact Info

Mimi Barbour:
www.mimibarbour.com
Twitter: @mimibarbour

Lorhainne Eckhart:
www.lorhainneeckhart.com
Twitter: @LEckhart

Sandy Hunter
www.sandrahunter.blogspot.com
Twitter: @FuroreScribindi

Genevieve McKay

W.J. Merritt
www.merrittsmuse.blogspot.com

Jim Miller
www.jamesmillermysterywriter.ca
Twitter: @JimMillerRabbi

Clive Scarff
www.clivescarff.com
Twitter: @clivescarff

Hendrik Witmans
www.qbwriter.blogspot.com

Writing in Progress Writers' Group
www.wipqb.com

10542008R10116

Made in the USA
Charleston, SC
12 December 2011